# Treasure Creek Dad
## Terri Reed

Steeple
Hill®

Published by Steeple Hill Books™

Special thanks and acknowledgment to Terri Reed for her
contribution to the Alaskan Bride Rush miniseries.

STEEPLE HILL BOOKS

Steeple
Hill®

Recycling programs
for this product may
not exist in your area.

ISBN-13: 978-0-373-81492-3

TREASURE CREEK DAD

**Printed in U.S.A.**

For I am confident of this very thing, that He who began a good work in you will perfect it until the day of Christ Jesus.
—*Philippians* 1:6

Thank you to my fellow Alaskan Bride Rush authors Jill, Janet, Debra, Brenda and Linda. It's been a pleasure working with you.

# Chapter One

"Tell me you've found him." Jake Rodgers planted his palms on the Treasure Creek, Alaska, police chief's desk and tried to keep the guilt and worry churning in his gut from spilling out. His friend Tucker Lawson was missing. And Jake should have done something to stop it.

Police Chief Reed Truscott's haggard expression bore concern and patience. "Jake, you'd be the first to know if we had. We've got search-and-rescue out. There just doesn't seem to be any trace of him."

Jake pushed away from the desk. Aggravation and distress burned in his chest. He should have been a better friend to Tucker during his father's passing. But Jake had been dealing with his own issues, and hadn't taken the time to console his friend or talk him out of the crazy idea of renting a plane and flying it across Alaska in search of solitude at some remote cabin.

Regret lay heavy on Jake's shoulders. He ran a hand through his hair, his short nails scraping along his scalp. "How can a plane just disappear? We're not in the Bermuda Triangle. This is Alaska, for crying out loud. And it isn't even snowing."

"My best guess is he got disoriented in the thunderstorm we had just after he left, and he headed in the wrong direction." Reed rubbed his jaw. "Thanks to your funding, we've expanded the search area. Even as we speak, Gage Parker is leading another search. All we can do now is wait."

"No, what we can do is pray," Jake countered, with a meaningful look at Reed, another friend he should have done better by.

Reed's mouth tipped upward in a rueful grimace. "Right. Good luck with that."

This was old ground—one Jake and Reed had covered before. Jake didn't understand Reed's ambivalence toward faith. For Jake, relying on his belief and trusting in God were the only things that had given him strength to survive the tumultuous years of his marriage, subsequent bitter divorce, and then later, struggling to balance his career and single parenthood after his ex-wife's death.

Deftly changing the subject, Reed said, "So your dad is finally giving you both reins of the family oil rigs?"

Jake sighed with a mixture of acceptance and anticipation. He'd left home vowing not to be like his parents, and now here he was hoping to carve out a life similar to theirs. "Looks like I'm going to be an oilman after all. He left me in charge of the whole shebang."

"How's Veronica taking the move?"

Reed's question layered more tension on Jake's already tightly strung shoulder muscles. "She's angry. We can barely have a civil conversation."

Reed shrugged. "She's twelve. And you moved her away from all her friends in Chicago—the only place she's ever known—to Podunk little Treasure Creek, which doesn't seem all that Podunk to you, because it was the only thing *you* knew growing up."

Of course he was right, but knowing that

didn't help. "Mom tells me Veronica is acting like a typical preteen, but I don't know."

"She is. She'll adjust."

"Hopefully sooner, rather than later." Jake pinched the bridge of his nose. "She's so addicted to her electronics, she hardly even steps outside."

"Why don't you take Veronica on a wilderness tour, using Amy's company?"

Amy James, one of Treasure Creek's more prominent citizens, owned and operated a company called Alaska's Treasures tour company. Hmm. *A guided wilderness tour.* The idea had merit.

Get Veronica out into the great outdoors, away from the television and the electronic gadgets she so loved. Some physical activity they could do together. Some father-daughter time away from all the distractions might be just the ticket to getting her to adjust to her new surroundings.

He'd have to confiscate her magazine stash. She'd fight him on it. Loudly. She'd start out hating the adventure, but maybe, by the end, she'd appreciate nature and come to accept their move. And he really wanted her to fall in love with the beauty and majesty of Alaska.

It had taken him moving away to realize the specialness of this part of the world.

"Do you think Amy would be willing to take us out?" Jake asked, knowing that Reed and Amy had a relationship of sorts. He wasn't sure of the particulars, but he knew Reed had proposed to the widow and was turned down.

Reed's brows drew together. "Actually, I think you'd do better to ask for Casey Donner."

"Why does that name ring a bell?"

"The Donner twins," Reed prompted.

"Oh, yeah. I remember them." Jake could picture the two girls, both with dark, curly hair, big blue eyes. One had been the prom queen while the other a tomboy. Each pretty in different ways.

Not that he'd ever dwelled on the fact. He'd been so set on leaving Treasure Creek that forming any ties, even with a pretty girl, was not something he allowed. He left town with a clear conscience. No broken hearts to come haunting him.

"I assume Casey is the tomboy?"

Reed grinned. "Yes. And she's a great gal. She'd be a good influence on Veronica. Very capable and levelheaded, just like her uncle Patrick. He taught that girl everything there is to know about nature before he passed."

Patrick Donner had been an icon in Treasure Creek when Jake was in high school. The original mountain man, tamed by two little girls. Jake remembered how scandalized the folks in town had been that Patrick would be caring for the orphaned twins when he spent so much time in the woods. But he'd surprised them all by taking in the girls and raising them right.

If Reed vouched for Casey, then that was good enough for Jake.

"You've sold me," Jake said, as he rose from the chair. "Thanks. And please, let me know the minute you hear anything about Tucker." His gut churned with anxiety and guilt. "I can't help but feel like something bad has happened to him."

Reed's jaw tightened. "We're doing our best to find him."

Contrition for questioning Reed's dedication arced through Jake. He knew they were both concerned about their friend. Jake couldn't shake the unease nipping at his mind. "I know. And I appreciate it."

Jake left the police station and headed up Treasure Creek Lane, the main thoroughfare. The weather was unseasonably warm for August, enough so that merchants had set up a few sidewalk displays for the flood of tourists, mostly female, that had recently descended upon Treasure Creek.

It wasn't the beauty of the scenery—all green trees, lush mountains with snowcapped peaks, and stunning vistas—or the quaint and rustic ambience of the town that had once thrived during the a booming Yukon gold rush of the late 1800s that had women flocking to this out-of-the-way Alaskan paradise. An article had appeared in some women's magazine, proclaiming that Treasure Creek men were looking for brides.

*Ha!* The last thing Jake was looking for was a bride. He'd done the marriage thing. No interest in going down that road again. All he wanted was to focus on raising Veronica and helping her become a productive human being, and then he wanted to live a quiet life, running the oil business his great-grandfather had started back in 1911.

He frowned and tried to analyze why that thought left him feeling hollow inside.

As he made his way toward the log cabin–style Alaska's Treasures office, he decided self-examination wasn't such a good thing. Not if the discontent rising to the surface was any indication.

He had to stay focused on what was important and within his control. His daughter and her well-being. He sent up a silent prayer that Casey Donner would be the answer.

Casey Donner fidgeted with the pencil as her boss, Amy James, a stunning, red-haired woman with a smattering of freckles and bright blue eyes, gave out the tour assignments for the month. So far, everyone had a tour planned.

Everyone except Casey. No one wanted a female guide. Not even the few men who'd come to town, hoping to cash in on the invasion of women.

Ever since that article came out in *Now Woman* magazine, Casey's work life had taken a nosedive. Women had swarmed Treasure Creek, hoping to hook one of the many eligible bachelors purported by the exposé to reside in town. Several of whom were part of the Alaska Treasures tour company's staff.

It didn't help that the article also stated that the company's lone female guide was not a threat to the converging women, because everyone in town—meaning said bachelors—considered Casey Donner to be "one of the guys".

Casey blew out an exasperated breath. So what if she was a tomboy, more comfortable in hiking boots and traipsing through the woods than wearing heels and throwing parties, like her twin sister, Amelia? The two were as different as night and day. If her sister were here, no one would claim she was "one of the guys."

God had made Casey this way. Who was she, or anyone else for that matter, to question the Almighty's decision?

Not that she talked with God much these days. An uncomfortable tinge of longing hit her. She mentally snuffed it out.

Over the past ten years she'd become comfortable with her life. She had a family in the tour company's staff and a mentor and friend in Amy. So really, what more could she ask for?

The door to the conference room opened

and the receptionist, Rachel Adams, poked her blond head inside.

Amy paused and smiled at Rachel. "Yes?"

"There's a gentleman here asking about a tour."

"Tell him I'll be right out," Amy answered.

"Actually, he wants to talk with Casey," Rachel replied, with a note of suppressed mirth.

Casey snapped to attention, as every set of eyes in the room zeroed in on her. Heat crept up her neck. "Who is it?"

Rachel flashed a grin. "Jake Rodgers."

Casey couldn't have heard right. Jake Rodgers was here asking for her? Of course she knew of the Rodgers family. They had started one of the first oil-drilling operations in the Treasure Creek area, back in the early nineteen hundreds.

She'd never had more than a passing conversation with Jake. He'd been two years ahead of her in high school, a star athlete and salutatorian of his class. He'd left Treasure Creek right after graduation, with a scholarship to some fancy college. He'd returned recently to take over his family's business, or so she'd inadvertently heard one day, while dining at Lizbet's Diner. She made it a personal rule not to be privy to the town gossip, most of which was inaccurate anyway. On that particular day, she'd been intrigued to hear Jake's name, but almost immediately caught herself and left the diner.

And now he was requesting to see Casey about a tour? Why her specifically? How did he even know she existed?

"May I?" Casey asked, nodding toward the door.

"By all means," Amy replied, with a smile that was both approving and encouraging.

Hastily, Casey left the conference room and halted in the hallway. Taking a few deep breaths to calm the sudden nervous jitters battering her stomach, she strove for a professional and detached demeanor. This was business, not personal. The man wanted a tour.

She paused in the waiting room doorway, aware that Rachel was avidly watching from behind her reception desk. Trying to keep her reaction from showing, Casey couldn't stop her heart from jumping a bit at the sight of Jake Rodgers.

He stood with his back to the door, staring out the large picture window that overlooked the main thoroughfare running the length of Treasure Creek. Tall, wide-shouldered and dressed impeccably in a navy business suit that attractively hugged his physique, he made Casey's breath catch.

Forcing her immediate reaction back to neutral, she cleared her throat before speaking. "Hello?"

He pivoted, making a stunning picture. The contrast of him in his business suit and the mountains rising in majestic peaks over the old gold-rush town, as his backdrop, somehow seemed right, like he was a man made to conquer the world. He'd been a heartthrob in high school, but now…a heartbreaker for sure.

His face had matured and become impossibly more striking, his jaw firmer, his cheekbones more pronounced. His dark, wavy hair was still thick and…*so* tempting.

Casey fought the sudden desire to run her fingers through his hair. Deep lines crinkled at the corners of his obsidian-colored eyes when he offered her a smile that knocked the air from her lungs.

He stepped closer and held hand out his hand. "Jake Rodgers. Not sure you remember me, but we went to high school together."

"I remember," she murmured. That was an understatement, if ever there was one. She hadn't realized how much of an impression he'd left on her.

Slipping her hand into his, she tried not to let the little shivers dancing up her arm go to her head. His hand was warm and smooth, his fingers strong, as they curled around her own. Yet, to her surprise, his hands weren't sissy hands. Though the short nails were clean, they weren't buffed by some manicurist, like some of the city men who visited Treasure Creek.

*Keep it professional, Donner.*

She extracted her hand. "What can I do for you, Mr. Rodgers?"

"Please, call me Jake. Reed Truscott suggested I hire you to take my daughter and me on a wilderness tour."

"Your daughter?" How had she missed that? Obviously, if she'd listened longer to the town gossips, she'd have known he had a child. "Your wife doesn't wish to come along?"

"I'm a single parent."

Her heart gave a squeeze of compassion, to think he was raising a daughter alone. She wondered about his marriage but was too polite to ask such an intimate question. But knowing he was single sent a little spark through her system. She wondered if he dated, or if being a single dad kept him unavailable.

Inwardly, she frowned at the direction her thoughts were taking. Since when had she decided she was ready to date again? Her heart was still smarting from her last attempt. She had no desire to go there again. She refocused her mind back to business. "How old is your daughter?"

"Twelve going on thirty," he said, with a rueful shake of his head.

She smiled at that assessment. "Did Reed suggest me specifically?"

Jake's dark eyes held her gaze. "Yes. He said you were one of the best, just like your uncle."

The mention of her late uncle caused a sharp pang of grief that never seemed to go away to hit her just below the breastbone. Absently, she rubbed the spot. Her uncle had been one of the original minds behind Alaska Treasures. Unfortunately, he never got to see the fruit of his ideas.

He succumbed to pancreatic cancer when Casey and Amelia were high school seniors. By becoming a guide herself, Casey honored her beloved uncle's memory.

"I'll have to thank Reed," Casey murmured, flattered by the recommendation. Yet, a wayward suspicion slithered through her mind. Had Amy set this up because Casey hadn't had any tours booked? She did not want anyone's pity.

"So, are you available?" Jake asked, his gaze searching her face. In more ways than she'd care to admit.

"What type of tour are you looking for?"

"Something to get my daughter out into nature, and hopefully give her a better appreciation for Alaska. She's not too happy that I moved us here from Chicago."

"Treasure Creek must seem like Nowheresville after the big city, but she'll come around. Our little part of the world is pretty awesome."

"But there's no mall or cool coffee shops," he stated with a shake of his head. Clearly, he'd heard that refrain from his daughter.

"The Java Joint has great coffee and cushy chairs for hanging out in. As for stores, well, there is The General Store. Carries a bit of everything." She shrugged. "I'm not too hip on big cities myself, so I can't really relate."

"Spoken like a true Alaskan," he said, with a grin.

"A transplanted Alaskan," she said, returning his smile.

She'd been born in San Francisco, where she'd lived until her parents died in a car accident. At the tender age of six, Casey and her twin were brought to live in Alaska with their late father's younger brother.

Casey had vague memories of her parents. The soft touch of her mother's hand, the melodic lullabies she would sing at night, and the excitement of daddy coming through the door at the end of the day. But mostly, Casey remembered the whizzing cars outside her bedroom window and the salty air of the bay.

She needed to change the subject before the overpowering sense of nostalgia building in her chest took root. She walked over to one of the side tables near the window and picked up a brochure. She flipped it open and held it out to him. "We have day hikes, backpacking trips ranging from two days to a week, water tours down the river, horseback-riding trips—"

He held up his hand. "Probably the backpacking, because Veronica's never ridden a horse and I don't do boats."

She cocked an eyebrow. "No sea legs, huh?"

"None whatsoever. I tried a cruise on Lake Michigan once. Not pretty," he stated, with a rueful shake of his head.

Casey liked how willing he was to accept his limitations. Not many men would admit to any weakness. "Okay, that narrows it down. How many days?"

He considered a moment. "A week?"

She eyed him a little closer. He looked in good shape, but that didn't mean he'd be up for the rigors of a week-long backpacking trip. "Just so you are aware, my trips are…" She searched for the right word. "*Rustic* at best. My tours are geared toward a true wilderness experience. We eat what we can carry, we fish when we hit the river and everyone helps set up and take down camp each day. We're up at sunrise and on the move all day until dusk. It's a pretty physical trip."

Raising an eyebrow in challenge, he said, "I think Veronica and I can handle that."

She shrugged, not quite sure he was correct. But…*his money, his call.*

"How soon would you like to go?"

"As soon as we can."

"Okay. We need to have time for orientation, when we'll go over the gear needed, safety tips. And I can answer any questions she or you might have. This meeting usually takes about an hour. Let's look at the calendar," she said, and moved to Rachel's desk. Rachel handed her the appointment book.

Casey flipped open to the month of August. Today was Wednesday, the fourth. "How about this coming Monday? Then we could do an orientation Friday evening, which would give you time over the weekend to get the supplies you and your daughter will require."

He didn't hesitate. "Great. My parents are leaving on Sunday after church for a week-long cruise, so this will work out perfect."

The door to the tour company blasted open,

and a tall, shapely woman bustled in, along with the cloying scent of liberally applied perfume. She wore a tailored pantsuit beneath a faux-fur long coat, stylish pumps with little rosesetts on the pointed tips and a Coach handbag slung over her shoulder. Clearly not a native to the area.

The woman paused a moment, as if assessing the situation, before gliding across the reception room and halting beside Casey. Dark brown hair, styled attractively around her oval face, made her sultry brown eyes stand out. Or maybe it was the curiosity that subtly shifted in her gaze, as she looked from Casey to Jake and back again.

Casey blinked, hardly believing what she was seeing. "Amelia?"

## Chapter Two

Not sure what to think of her sister's sudden and unexpected appearance after so many years away, Casey asked, "What are you doing here?"

Raising a perfectly plucked eyebrow, Amelia said, "Hello to you, too, sis."

"Sorry. Hi." Casey gave Amelia an awkward hug.

As Amelia released Casey, she tugged on Casey's short ponytail. "I came for our class reunion, of course. And because I saw that wonderful article about Treasure Creek and all the hunky bachelors." She slid a glance toward Jake.

A wave of irritation crashed over Casey, but with Jake watching, she choose to ignore the reminder of that awful article, as well as her sister's condescending action and the tone that suggested Casey should have known why she'd returned.

But how could Casey possibly know her twin would come back for the reunion, when Amelia hadn't even RSVPed? Since Casey was on the reunion decoration committee even though she wasn't planning to attend, she'd heard all about how her sister hadn't responded yet. "The reunion's not for another three weeks."

Amelia shrugged and said, in an airy tone, "I had some vacation time I needed to use or lose, so I thought I'd come early."

"Okay." That sounded reasonable. Or did it?

If it were anyone other than Amelia, Casey would believe the explanation. But this was Amelia talking—the girl who had left two days after they'd graduated from high school, loudly proclaiming she couldn't wait to get as far away as she could from Treasure Creek. She'd ended up in San Francisco. Back to the place where they were born.

Over the last decade, though she called every few weeks, she'd come back only twice.

Each time staying no more than a couple of days before declaring she couldn't take another minute in this small town. So why the sudden need to return? And from the sound of it, for an extended stay.

Casey knew she should be glad to see her sister, but for some reason, Amelia's presence only stirred up annoyance. How awful was that? Guilt curled in Casey's belly, making her breakfast churn.

A chiming noise emanated from Amelia's purse. She stuck her hand inside and silenced the cell phone.

"You're not going to answer that?" Casey asked, curious as to why she wouldn't.

"No." Amelia turned her red, glossy smile on Jake. "Jake Rodgers, right?" She held out her soft-looking, manicured hand. "I remember you. You were ahead of us by a couple of years." Her gaze slid speculatively to Casey and then back to Jake. "I didn't know you two were friends."

The insinuation in her voice grated across Casey's nerves. "He's my client," she said, trying to keep impatience out of her tone.

Jake briefly shook her offered hand. "Nice

to meet you, Amelia. I take it you don't live in Treasure Creek anymore."

"Oh, please. No, I flew the coop after graduation. Just like you. I ended up in San Francisco. I manage a department store now," she said, with obvious pride in her voice. "Where did you end up?"

"The windy city of Chicago."

"Ah. And now you're back." Her dark eyes took on a predatory gleam. "For how long?"

Casey clenched her jaw at her sister's obvious ploy. Amelia liked her men rich, which Jake Rodgers definitely was.

"Permanently," Jake stated, firmly. "I'm taking over the family business.

"How interesting." She glanced at Casey. "So you're hiring my sis to take you on a wilderness tour? Very exciting."

Jake flashed a grin at Casey. "Yes, I am. We were discussing the details."

Amelia bumped Casey with her shoulder. "I've always wanted to take one of sis's tours, but have never had the time. Until now."

Right. Like Casey believed that. Her prissy sister wouldn't last ten minutes out in the Alaskan wilderness. Needing to get her sister out of her hair so she could finish up with

Jake, Casey dug her house keys from the side pocket of her hiking pants and held them out. "Why don't you take my keys and head to the house? You can unpack and unwind. I'll be home later."

Ignoring the dangling keys hanging from Casey's finger, Amelia pinned her with a challenging look. "I'd really like to hear about this tour. When are you going?" She slanted a coy glance at Jake. "Is there room for one more?"

"We haven't firmed up the particulars. We were talking about leaving this coming Monday." Jake tilted his head and shifted his gaze to Casey. "I'm open to having a group tour."

Dread sluiced through Casey like a dam bursting. Gritting her teeth in a semblance of what she hoped was a smile, Casey said to Jake, "That's very generous of you." To her sister, she said, "Amelia, it's a backpacking trip. You know? Hiking through the woods, climbing over rough terrain, camping out, carrying your own equipment."

"Oh, how rugged that sounds." Amelia grinned, flashing her even, blindingly white teeth. "I love it. Count me in."

"Great." *Just great…not.*

Well, so much for finding out if she had a shot with Jake. With Amelia around, Casey didn't stand a chance. For as long as Casey could remember, people gravitated to Amelia, leaving Casey to follow in her shadow. Why would Jake be any different?

It was just as well, Casey reasoned. She had experienced too much loss to ever want to risk her heart to love again.

Not even for the handsome, charming Jake Rodgers.

"No way. That sounds horrible."

Jake stared at his daughter slouched on the navy leather couch of his parents' home. She hadn't even looked up from the fashion magazine in her lap when he'd told her of the plans. She just kept cutting away with the scissors. Strewn all over the couch were cutouts from the various magazines stacked on the floor. Veronica dreamed of being a fashion model or designer or some such. She pasted the cutouts onto a big piece of poster board in her room.

His jaw tightened and he tried to keep impatience from edging his tone. "This isn't up for debate, Veronica. We are going on this backpacking trip next week."

She snapped the magazine closed and rose to her feet. Tall for her age, she was willowy, with porcelain features like her mother. Her straight, strawberry-blond hair fell past her shoulders. "Fine. Whatever. Like I have any choice."

"You have a choice—to enjoy this trip. Or you can choose to be miserable. You are in control of your attitude."

The tight-leg designer jeans and frilly blouse she wore had been purchased back in Chicago, where they were the norm. Here in Treasure Creek, she looked out of place. The other kids Jake had seen around town wore more rugged clothing, better suited to life in Alaska. "Why don't we go shopping for more appropriate attire for the trip? You'll need some sweatshirts, T-shirts and jeans you can actually move in."

"Dad!" She rolled her hazel eyes, gathered her clippings, and stomped out of the living room and down the hall to her bedroom, which used to be Jake's when he was a teen. He now slept in the guest room. He cringed when Veronica slammed the door shut. Should he discipline her for the rude behavior?

He wished kids came with a manual. Being a single parent wasn't exactly how he'd planned his life. But Natalie was gone, so he was doing the best he could.

Was he making a mistake to insist on the trip? It had seemed like such a good idea when Reed suggested it. After talking with Casey, whose friendly demeanor and down-to-earth attitude had been a refreshing change from the city women he'd become accustomed to, he'd been convinced he was making the right decision. Especially after Casey's sister had shown up wanting to be a part of the tour.

Here were two very different women, yet each seemed so confident and success-ful. Surely the influence of these two con-trasting females would be a good thing for Veronica.

And Jake had to admit, from the moment he'd seen Casey Donner in the reflection of the window in the reception room, looking so adorable in cargo pants, a form-fitting zip-up jacket and with her dark hair pulled back from her unadorned face, he'd been intrigued.

Most females looked at him with dollar

signs in their eyes, just as Amelia Donner had the second she'd walked into the tour company office. But not Casey.

There had been such lively intelligence in Casey's dark eyes. And when she'd looked him up and down, assessing his stamina for the backpacking trip and finding him wanting, he'd been swamped with the need to prove her wrong. A sensation he hadn't experienced in a long time.

"Did you put Reed up to suggesting me to Jake for this tour?" Casey asked, watching her friend, Amy, closely over the expanse of the oak desk in her boss's office. This was the first opportunity Casey had had to talk alone with Amy since yesterday.

Amy blinked, her blues eyes guileless. "No. Why would you think I had?"

Feeling guilty for suspecting her friend of pitying her, Casey said, "It just was so out of the blue."

Mouth quirking, Amy said, "Like your sister's return was out of the blue?"

"Yeah. What's up with that? She said she's here for the reunion. But three weeks early? Something's up."

"Have you asked her about it?"

"Not really," Casey said, a bit sheepishly. "We don't have the kind of relationship that most twins do. Or at least, we haven't since we moved to Alaska. Everything changed. She shut me out."

"That must have hurt," Amy said, in a gentle tone. It had.

"I got over it."

Amy steepled her fingers on the desk. "Her joining the Rodgers tour might be a really good thing, then. You two might grow closer."

Of course Amy would think of the situation as an opportunity for the sisters to bond. Amy was an idealist in many ways. Casey, not so much.

"It's just so infuriating that my sister would weasel her way in like this," Casey said, sure that Amelia's motivation had nothing to do with a desire to be out in nature and everything to do with Jake. Not that that was any of Casey's concern. "Who is Amelia kidding? She'll hate it and make everyone miserable."

Amy slipped off her serviceable clogs and propped her sock-clad feet on the arm of her chair. Little penguins, dressed in frilly outfits, marched up the sides of her long, white socks and disappeared beneath the legs of Amy's khaki pants. "Give her a chance. She may have changed."

Casey scoffed. "If the way Amelia's taken over the house is any indication, no, she hasn't. Her stuff is everywhere." Jamming her hands into the pockets of her hooded sweatshirt, Casey slunk further in her chair. "My bathroom now reeks of some flowery perfume that makes me sneeze every time I go in."

"She does kind of apply a lot," Amy said, with a grin. "But a stinky sister isn't what's really bothering you, is it?"

It was so like Amy to see to the heart of a matter. Casey groaned. "No, it isn't."

"Come on, tell me," Amy cajoled.

"It's just that article and…oh, I don't know." She hated to come across as whiney and ungrateful. How did she explain this growing discontentment gnawing away at her nicely ordered life?

It wasn't even the fact that she was the brunt of so many jokes since that article came out—though the snickering *was* getting old. What bothered her most was that, deep inside she felt hollow, empty. Like something was missing.

Her gaze snagged on a framed photo of Amy and her late husband, Ben, and their two boys. What a beautiful family. They looked so happy.

That's what Casey wanted. A family of her own. A love like Amy and Ben had shared. She held tight to the knowledge that their love proved love existed.

An uninvited memory escaped from the recesses of her mind and tore across her brain, reminding her that love came with a price. A price she'd paid once. A price that left her wounded and discouraged.

She slapped the memory down and stuffed it back into its box inside her head, and refocused on the grief of her friend's loss.

Amy searched her face, as if she sensed her pain. "I'm sorry that article has caused you hurt."

Casey waved away Amy's self-imposed guilt. "I don't blame you. And it's really the truth. I'm 'one of guys.'" She made air quotes to emphasize her words.

"A role that you've perpetuated. You keep everyone at arm's length. I think it's time for you to stop keeping yourself so isolated. Be open to a relationship."

"But the risk is too great," Casey murmured. She didn't want to lose someone she loved again. She'd lost her parents, Uncle Patrick and, essentially, Amelia. Another name floated into her consciousness. She ignored it.

Amy gave her a sad, direct look and said softly, "I know. But the risk is worth it, Casey. I wouldn't trade one single ounce of heartache if it meant not having ever loved Ben."

Ouch. Direct hit. "Just rip my heart out and feed it to me, why don't you, Amy?"

Amy's lips twitched. "Hey, if you didn't want the truth, you wouldn't be sitting here."

Casey sighed. "I know. You've never pulled any punches with me, and I appreciate it."

"Jake Rodgers doesn't think of you as 'one of the guys,'" Amy stated, with a curving of her lips, as she mimicked Casey's air quotes.

"Not yet, maybe, but give him time." Casey rolled her eyes. "I'm not his type, anyway."

"And you know this *how?*"

"He's a city guy now, regardless that he was

born here. And in case you haven't noticed, I'm not exactly a beauty queen. Amelia's more his type. Glamor and glitz. Besides," Casey pointed out, "he's a single dad trying to raise his daughter. What do I know about kids?"

Amy gave her a chiding look. "Casey, you're great with kids. The boys love you. And you've dealt with children on several tours and did great, so don't use his daughter as an excuse to keep him at arm's length."

"But I'm no good at the dating thing." She cringed, remembering the last date she'd been on.

Bucky Holland, the town's mechanic and one of the town's many bachelors, had invited her to dinner at Martelli's, a fancy grill in town. Casey had looked forward to the date with hopeful anticipation. Maybe this time a date would end differently.

But the evening had consisted of forced conversation and awkward silences. When he dropped her off and roared away in his big rig—faster than if a bear had been chasing him—she'd decided dating wasn't her thing.

"Just be yourself, Casey. If a relationship with Jake or any other man is part of God's plan for your life, then everything will work out, regardless of your sister or that article."

Tugging on her bottom lip, Casey wished she shared Amy's convictions. But trusting God was something Casey couldn't do. Not ever again. A blast of anger blew through her. She'd trusted that God would answer her prayers and make Uncle Patrick well. God hadn't. She'd trusted God to protect her heart when Seth came into her life. Another prayer ignored.

There was a knock at the door. "Come in," Amy called.

Rachel stepped inside. "The police chief is here to see you, Amy."

"Tell Reed I'll be a moment longer," Amy said, her voice taking on a slight edge.

Anticipation? Or irritation?

When Rachel shut the door, Casey raised an eyebrow. "A social call?"

Amy brushed a lock of red hair back behind her ear. Beneath her smattering of freckles, a blush brightened her cheeks. "No. We don't have that kind of relationship. I'm sure there's some official reason he's stopping by."

Glancing at the photo on the desk, Casey knew Ben would want Amy to find love again.

Rising from her seat, Casey said, "He's a good man, Amy. Ben wouldn't mind."

Amy frowned, as a shadow of sorrow passed over her expression. "Now who's ripping whose heart out?"

Casey held up her hands in a show of entreaty. "Sorry. Not another word."

"Thank you." Amy rose and rounded the desk, to put her arm around Casey's shoulders. "It's all going to work out. Be open to what God has in store for you."

Casey hugged Amy for a moment, thankful to have such a wise and gracious friend. After Patrick died, Amy and her late husband had taken Casey under their wing. Casey would be forever grateful to Ben James for taking a chance and hiring her as a wilderness guide. She missed him, as did everyone in Treasure Creek. He'd been the mayor as well as the owner of Alaska's Treasures.

His death had been a tragic accident. Ben had been trying to save the life of a client during a dangerous rapids trip and lost his life for the effort. Reed Truscott had witnessed the devastating event. Perhaps that was the tension Casey always sensed between Amy and Reed.

As Casey left Amy's office, she glanced at her watch and decided she could still get a ten-mile run in before she went home. She met Reed in the hall. "Hey, Chief. Thank you for recommending me to Jake Rodgers."

Reed nodded in acknowledgement but didn't slow down. "No thanks necessary. You'll be good for Jake." He disappeared inside Amy's office.

Okay. Not the most cordial person, but he got the job done. Just why did Chief Truscott think Casey would be good for Jake?

Casey opened the front door to the small A-frame house that she'd lived in since she'd first come to Alaska twenty-two years ago. To a little girl who'd just lost her parents, the house had seemed big and strange, so very different than her parents' turn-of-the-century town house in the heart of San Francisco. Now the A-frame was comfortable, her safe haven.

At least it had been, until Amelia returned.

Casey stepped across the threshold to the darkened living room and tension crept up her neck. Had Amelia left as mysteriously as she'd returned?

A movement to her right jolted her system. She pivoted, prepared to defend herself against an attack. But none came.

She reached out to flip on the light switch. The table lamp by the couch glowed, throwing shadows around the room. Casey blinked as her eyes adjusted. Her sister sat in the rocker by the window.

A sense of déjà vu swept over Casey. Many times, when Casey and Uncle Patrick had returned from some adventure out in the wilderness, they would find Amelia quietly sitting in the rocker, waiting for them as she now waited for Casey. Casey had never understood why Amelia had chosen to stay home alone while she and Patrick went exploring.

Were those tears wetting her sister's lashes? "Amelia? Are you okay?"

"Of course. Why wouldn't I be?" Amelia snapped, and rose from the chair to glide past Casey toward the kitchen. She wore a turquoise top with a matching skirt that flowed with each step. "Dinner is ready."

Casey closed the front door and went to the sink to wash her hands. "Thanks for cooking. You know, you don't have to take care of me."

"I know I don't have to," Amelia said as she set on the table a plate with little canapés. "But what else is there to do in this town but cook? Besides, I didn't make anything fancy, because your cupboards are pathetic."

"I haven't gone shopping this week." Taking the seat opposite Amelia, Casey eyed the plate of crostini topped with pepperoni and stuffed olives. This was dinner? Casey's stomach growled. "And there's plenty to do."

"Like?"

The ring of Amelia's cell phone drew Casey's attention. Amelia didn't move. "Aren't you going to pick up?"

Amelia made a face. "No."

"Do you want to talk about it?" Casey asked, wondering at her sister's odd behavior.

"No." Amelia made a rolling gesture with her hand. "You were saying what there was to do in town."

*Pursue Jake?*

Not wanting to put that idea into Amelia's head, Casey said, "You could browse the shops. Take a walk. Volunteer to help with the reunion committee."

Amelia plucked a crostini from the plate and held it between her two fingers as if she were holding fine china. "Now, that sounds perfect for my skill set. Who do I talk to about helping with the committee?"

"Renee Haversham. I can introduce you when we get back from our backpacking trip." Casey searched her sister's face closely. In some ways it was like looking in a mirror, but not. To Casey, Amelia's pale complexion was flawless, her eyes bluer and her features better proportioned. Was it any wonder people, men especially, gravitated to Amelia? "Unless you've changed your mind about going?"

"No, I haven't." Amelia peered at her just as closely. "You don't want me to go, do you?"

Stalling as she tried to think how best to answer her twin, Casey popped a crostini into her mouth and chewed slowly. After she'd swallowed and taken a sip of water, she said, "It's not that I don't want you to go—I just can't see you enjoying backpacking."

With a shrug, Amelia said, "We'll see. Having Jake Rodgers along should be interesting. I understand he's available." She rubbed her hands together. "One of those bachelors that magazine talked about."

Casey's stomach clenched, and it wasn't from the spicy pepperoni. "He's single."

"Divorced," she corrected. "And rich. Just the kind of guy I like."

The speculative gleam in her twin's gaze made Casey's mouth go dry. She took a quick sip of water before saying, "Amelia, don't play with Jake's affections. He's struggling right now to raise his daughter. He doesn't need you coming on strong with no intention of following through."

Amelia's expression darkened. "How do you know I wouldn't follow through?"

"You left a string of broken hearts behind when you charged out of Treasure Creek." And who knew how many men she'd caught and thrown away in San Francisco? Every time Amelia called home, she'd spoken of someone new. "You never follow through. At least not when it comes to love."

"Oh, and you're some expert? When have you ever been in love?"

The barb hit home. "Seth Davenport," Casey replied just a tad too defensively for her liking.

Amelia scoffed. "Right. You had one date with the nerd. That doesn't qualify."

It had been more than just one date. But Casey wasn't about to share with her twin the intimate details of her disastrous romance, though she cringed to associate the nicety of romance with what had transpired between her and Seth.

Switching gears to keep the focus off herself, Casey said, "Why are you really home?"

Amelia arched one perfectly waxed eyebrow—her signature expression that drove Casey nuts. "Excuse me?"

Casey reached across the table and took Amelia's hand. "Don't pretend not to understand me. Why did you return home so early? And why were you crying when I came in?"

Her expression shut down as she extracted her hand from Casey's hold. "I'll leave if you don't want me here."

Frustration bounced around Casey's chest. Amelia always did that—twisted Casey's words around and used them against her. "I didn't say that."

"Good." Amelia took her plate to the sink and began doing the dishes, leaving Casey's questions unanswered.

Her sister was hiding something. Casey wasn't sure how to get Amelia to open up. She wasn't even sure she wanted to try. Amy's voice rang in her head, urging her to give Amelia a chance. They might grow closer. Maybe close enough for Amelia to confide in her. Because whatever Amelia wasn't saying was upsetting her.

# Chapter Three

"Welcome, everyone," Casey said, her gaze roaming over the six people assembled in the prep room of Alaska's Treasures tour company. Once word had gone out that another tour had opened slots, three more people signed up. An older married couple, newly retired to Treasure Creek, Doug and Marie Caruthers, and a freelance photojournalist, Stan Ford.

Casey's gaze snagged on Jake. He wore a pale yellow-colored pullover sweater that heightened the darkness of his hair and eyes. Faded jeans hugged his long, lean legs. She met his gaze. He stared back with polite attention. But then his eyes seemed to darken and his mouth curved into a charming smile. Her pulse quickened, nearly making her lose her train of thought. She wondered what his face—his eyes—would look like across the warm light from a camp fire. Would he still look at her so intently? Could his interest ever be more than just guide and client? Did she want it, too?

Casey forced herself to keep her gaze moving. Jake's daughter, on the other hand, made it clear by her crossed arms and bored expression that she wanted to be anywhere but here. Her fuzzy coat and bright-colored leggings wouldn't work on this trip, but they certainly made her stand out from the crowd. Casey hoped the tall, strawberry-blonde and delicately pretty child would have the stamina to make the long journey. Casey would keep an extra-alert eye on Veronica.

"I'm Casey Donner, your guide for this tour. The emphasis of our trip will be making sure each of you garners the most enjoyment of your Alaska's Treasures tour experience."

She gestured to the long metal table behind her, where she'd laid out a backpack and everything that would need to go inside. "As you can see from the items on this table, there is a lot of equipment that will be brought with us. Goods and services included in your adventure are food, cooking equipment and safety gear. We spread the weight out through everyone's backpacks so that no one person's pack is too heavy."

She picked up a stack of papers from the chair to her side. "Each of you will receive a packet with a checklist of the items you'll need to provide for yourself. Give careful consideration to clothing. Fabrics that wick moisture away from the body and dry quickly are preferable. One thing you should keep in mind is how much hiking you'll be doing, so good shoe wear is essential."

"Will regular tennis shoes suffice?" Stan asked, as he lifted the camera slung around his neck and snapped off some pictures of Casey.

Disconcerted by the camera, Casey looked away as she answered. "I'd suggest hiking boots."

"Like yours?" Marie asked, her green eyes wide, in a face lightly lined with age. She and her husband were in their sixties but could pass for much younger.

Casey lifted her foot to show her worn, clunky boots. "Yes, like these. Something waterproof and with a good tread."

"They're ugly," groused Veronica, her vivid blues hostile as she stared at Casey.

Casey blinked in surprise that the girl had even heard the conversation, with her earbuds blasting whatever she'd loaded on her attached iPod.

"Veronica, be polite." Jake admonished the girl with an apologetic glance at Casey.

Casey made a gesture for him not to worry about his daughter's rudeness.

"I agree," Amelia said. She stood slightly apart from the rest of the group and looked regal in her designer stretch pants and frilly top. She'd taken off the shearling jacket she'd arrived in. "Do they come in colors other than brown?"

Holding on to her patience and trying not to take Veronica's dark looks personally, Casey said, "I'm not sure. You can purchase boots at The General Store on Treasure Creek Lane."

Amelia moved to stand near one end of the table. Her bangle bracelets clinked as she gestured. "We have to carry all of this stuff?"

"Yes, you do."

Amelia picked up a freeze-dried dinner package. "What's this?"

Suppressing a smile, Casey said, "Food."

Amelia made a face. "You're kidding, right?"

"Nope. Each pack will hold a little over eight pounds of food that will last for the seven days we're out."

"Wait," Amelia said, her gaze narrowing. "We don't have a pack mule, or something, to carry our food?"

Casey shook her head, sure now Amelia would back out. "No. This isn't *City Slickers*, the Alaska version. This is the real deal."

Looking almost green, Amelia stepped away from the table.

Turning back to the others, Casey said, "We'll be walking four to six miles a day, making camp each night. We'll loop around the Chilkoot trail, crossing through some mountainous territory and skirting along the Taiya River, where you'll get a chance to do some fishing. We should have mild weather, with the high temp in the midsixties and lows at night in the thirties or forties. But everyone should be prepared for rain, as well."

"Just kill me now," Veronica groaned. "I can't walk that much."

"You'll do fine," Jake said, between clenched teeth.

Casey smiled at Veronica. "Don't worry. We'll take breaks and have plenty of time to savor the breathtaking views."

"Oh, goody," Veronica replied, her tone full of sarcasm.

Amelia sidled up to Jake and Veronica. "Stick with me, kid. We'll make it happen."

Veronica's gaze narrowed. "Did you make your necklace?"

Seemingly unfazed by Veronica's surly tone, Amelia touched the gold, beaded trinket at her neck and arched her eyebrow. "No. This a Marc Antonio original. Worth way more than that iPod you're attached to."

Veronica blinked. "Oh, a Marc Antonio? Wow."

Casey couldn't believe it. The kid hadn't even flinched at the insult, and was impressed by her sister's gaudy jewelry. Casey didn't even know who Marc—whatever—was.

Forcing her attention back to the orientation, Casey talked about the trip a bit more, showed some slides highlighting points from past trips and then answered questions. When everyone was satisfied and had taken a packet of necessary information, Casey headed over to Jake and his daughter, hoping to connect with the kid. Jake seemed to be having a hard time with the preteen as they conversed near the door. Veronica's pretty face was pulled into a sullen pout as she stared at her father's feet—while he bent to catch her eye.

"Remember what I told you. How you experience this is up to you," Jake was saying as Casey approached.

Veronica snorted.

Jake glanced Casey's way and straightened. His beleaguered expression tugged at Casey's heart. She could tell he was really trying. Not that she had much experience with adolescents, but she wanted to reach out to Jake and his daughter just the same.

"It won't be as awful as you're anticipating," Casey said.

Veronica didn't look up. "Yes, it will."

"Veron—"

Casey held up her hand to cut off his words. "I remember the first time I went out on a full-blown backpacking trip. I was about your age when my uncle loaded me up with a pack that weighed more than I did. I'll admit, in the beginning it was very tiring and I was sure I couldn't go on, but after a while you get into a rhythm."

"Like a conga line?" Amelia asked, as she joined them. "I can get into that." She started doing the conga, rolling her arms, kicking her feet out to the side.

Casey blinked in surprise to see her sister, usually so very staid and controlled, act so goofy. And even more surprising was the tug of a smile on Veronica's face.

"Well, I don't know about the conga, but it will be fun," Casey said.

"I'm looking forward to being out in nature and away from all the electronics," Jake said, his gaze directed at Casey.

"Whoa. What? No electronics?" Veronica looked scandalized.

"No electronics," Jake stated, firmly.

"You won't miss them. I promise," Casey interjected.

The grateful and approving look Jake sent her way made her cheeks heat up.

"No iPod even?" Amelia asked, looking nearly as traumatized by the prospect.

Jake slanted her a cutting glance. "Nothing."

Amelia and Veronica shared a long-suffering look.

"Can I talk to you?" Casey took her sister by the arm and led her away before she had time to protest.

"Don't do that," Casey said, keeping her voice low as they halted a few feet away.

"Do what?"

"Undermine Jake with his daughter."

Amelia gave her a look that clearly said she thought Casey was nuts. "Please. I wasn't. When did you become Miss Goody Two-shoes, anyway?"

Casey frowned, stung by that assessment. "I'm not." At least she'd never thought of herself that way. She had responsibilities, and she took them seriously. Uncle Patrick had taught her the importance of that.

Amelia rolled her eyes. "Whatever." She walked away and headed straight back to Jake and his daughter.

Casey had a sinking feeling Amelia was trying to worm her way into Jake's heart through his daughter. A few minutes later, Amelia called out to Casey. "Hey, sis, we're heading over to Lizbet's for milkshakes. You want to come with us?"

She did, with everything in her. But it was her responsibility to put away the orientation gear and close up the tour company. Trying to keep her disappointment and frustration from echoing in her voice, she said as neutrally as she could, "I've got to close up."

"Okay, then," Amelia said, with a satisfied smile, before she walked out the door with Veronica following closely behind.

Jake strode over to where Casey stood. Her heart fluttered at his closeness. "Come to Lizbet's when you're done," he said.

Liking that he'd think to make the suggestion, Casey nodded. "I'll will. Thank you."

He held the packet of information up. "There's an awful lot of stuff here. Would you be willing to help Veronica and me purchase everything we need?"

Thrilled by the request, she tried to keep excitement out of her voice. "Of course. I'd love to."

He grinned. "Great. How about tomorrow morning?"

"Perfect."

"You're the best." He saluted and jogged away.

"The best," she repeated, though inside her

head the refrain "one of the guys" mocked her. Did Jake see her as "one of the guys"?

And did she care?

Jake stirred his melting chocolate milkshake while his daughter and Amelia chatted nonstop about fashion and makeup. He'd long since tuned them out, staring through the front window of Lizbet's Diner. At least he had a view of the main street through Treasure Creek to occupy his attention.

He wasn't keeping watch for Casey to join them for milkshakes. He really wasn't. He'd heard she was a serious loner. Way too independent, too self-sufficient to ever want a family. So not his type.

Behind him the little restaurant buzzed with activity. It was a Friday night, after all. Lots of people were out for a bite to eat, or, like the three of them, here for one of Lizbet's delicious milkshakes. The rustic eatery, with its wooden tables and benches, plank floors and mason jars filled with flowers as centerpieces, was a popular hangout for the locals. The menu ranged from good old-fashioned hamburgers and fries to more fancy salmon steaks, to basic breakfast fare, which they served all day.

Jake glanced at his watch. Forty-five minutes. Did it really take Casey that long to close up the tour offices?

"Do you have somewhere to be?" Amelia asked.

Jerking his gaze to Amelia's lively blue eyes, Jake felt heat rise up his neck. He'd made it too obvious that he was bored. "It's getting late," he said, inanely.

"Dad, it's not even nine o'clock," Veronica whined, with a toss of her long mane. "And tomorrow's Saturday."

Old pain rippled through his heart. The way Veronica flipped her hair was so reminiscent of Natalie. Amazing how Veronica shared so many of her mother's physical gestures, even though she was an infant when Natalie left. Genes were powerful things.

"Yeah, Jake. Tomorrow's a sleep-in day," Amelia interjected, with a mocking tone.

"Fine. We can stay a little longer," Jake said, at a loss as to why he was so antsy.

Amelia gave him a regal smile. She really was a pretty woman, Jake thought.

Very polished and striking. He'd watched several male heads turn when they'd entered the diner. His daughter certainly had taken a shine to Amelia, once Veronica discovered their common interest in fashion. He couldn't believe his luck.

Thank goodness Amelia had elected to join their tour. He thought she'd be a good influence on Veronica. Amelia related well to his daughter, and it seemed like she would be a good role model, considering she actually had a paying job in the fashion industry that fascinated Veronica so much.

A strange sensation pricked the back of his neck and he looked out the window. His gaze collided with Casey's. The prickle at his neck became a buzz that shot through him. Man, she'd startled him. She was standing on the sidewalk outside the restaurant. He raised his hand to wave her inside, but she was already turning away and hurrying down the street.

Why was she leaving? And what was that odd expression on her lovely face? She looked…upset.

Abruptly, Jake stood, startling Amelia and Veronica. "I'll be right back," he said, and rushed out of the diner.

* * *

Casey moved down Treasure Creek Lane at a fast clip, passing the carefully designed building façades that created a feel of an era long past. In its heyday, Treasure Creek had been a booming gold-rush town, because its location made a perfect point for prospectors to embark from on their quest for gold up the Chilkoot and White Pass trails.

Tonight however, Casey's quest was to nurse her wounded pride in the privacy of her own home, before her sister returned. How silly of Casey to think that joining Jake, Amelia and Veronica was a good idea. From the way Jake and Amelia were making moon eyes at each other, Casey knew there was no room for her in the equation. Her heart squeezed tight.

Why that hurt so much she didn't know. Well, okay maybe she did know. Jake had gone out of his way to make sure she'd been included, and had even asked for her to help in acquiring the appropriate gear for their upcoming tour. She'd let that attention go to her head. She'd let herself believe he was interested in her.

Of course he'd gravitate to Amelia. Everyone did. Casey really shouldn't be concerned that Jake would get hurt by her twin. The man was an adult. He could take care of himself.

But still…Casey sighed and silently chanted, "Not my problem. Not my problem."

She would get through this tour by keeping things professional and detached. And by locking her heart up tight. It had always worked in the past.

She veered left and crossed the street, barely slowing to allow a car to pass. She picked up her pace and had made it halfway down the block when someone grabbed her elbow from behind.

"Hey," she yelped, and wrenched her arm away, preparing to strike out. She blinked in stunned surprise to see Jake standing next to her, bathed in the glow of the streetlamp. Light reflected off his dark hair and kissed the angular planes of his handsome face. He jammed his hands into the pockets of his jeans, stretching the pale yellow-colored pullover across his muscular chest.

"Whew, woman. You can hustle. Didn't you hear me calling your name?" Jake asked, sounding a bit winded.

"No. I guess I was lost in thought," she

said, relaxing her stance. "What are you doing here? Where's Amelia and Veronica?"

"They're still at Lizbet's. I saw you through the window. Why didn't you come in?"

*Ugh.* She'd hoped he hadn't noticed her standing there, gawking at them. Like an outsider looking in. "It's late." She scrambled for a reasonable explanation. "I figured you all were about done anyway."

"We'd have still welcomed you," he said, studying her face. "The orientation went well. I'm excited about this trip. And thank you for your willingness to help us shop tomorrow. I think it will be a good experience for Veronica and me."

She smiled. "That's my goal." Nothing more.

*Right?*

The door to the church opened. Pastor Ed Michaels and his wife, Jenny, stepped out. Grateful for the interruption to the embarrassing encounter, Casey waved. She really liked the forty-something couple, even if she didn't regularly attend services. Pastor Ed locked the door and then escorted his wife down the walkway.

"Good evening, Casey," Pastor Ed said.

"Jake." The two men shook hands. "Have you met my wife, Jenny?"

"Nice to meet you," Jake said.

Jenny, a petite brunette with a sunny disposition, smiled back. "Hello." Her gaze bounced back and forth between Jake and Casey. "What are you two up to this evening?"

Casey nearly groaned aloud. The last thing she needed was for the pastor and his wife to think she and Jake were dating, when that couldn't be farther from the truth. News like that traveled fast in a small town, and if she didn't nip in the bud now, everyone would have them hitched and setting up housekeeping before she knew it.

Helping Jake shop tomorrow didn't count. That was business. Nothing more.

"My daughter and I are taking a guided tour with Casey in a couple of days. Casey has graciously agreed to help us pick out our backpacks tomorrow, and we were discussing that."

Casey could have hugged Jake for explaining their association so succinctly.

Jenny looked up at her husband, who stood a good foot taller than she. "We should take a guided tour sometime."

"We should," Ed agreed. Though he was not classically handsome, there was something very appealing about the pastor. His nose was a bit too big for his face, but his eyes were kind and his crooked smile was endearing.

"I'd love to take you out on the trail sometime. Just say when," Casey offered.

"That's kind of you to offer, Casey. We'll have to look at our calendars," Pastor Ed said.

"Will we see you two tomorrow at the barbeque?" Jenny asked, her gaze a bit too pointed for Casey's liking. What a little matchmaker!

Casey hadn't ever attended the church's weekly singles group. She didn't want to be put out on display or be seen as desperate. It was bad enough to be labeled "one of the guys," but to actually advertise that she was unattached by going to a singles group just didn't appeal.

"Barbeque?" Jake inquired.

"Every week we have a Saturday-night singles social. Since the weather has been so mild we've had a barbeque. It's a fun time. Mostly fellowship, with a bit of worship time.

Nothing formal," Pastor Ed explained. "We'd love for you both to join us."

"That sounds great," Jake said, and turned to Casey. "What do you think? Are you free tomorrow night?"

Just when Casey managed to shove away hopes of Jake being interested in her, Jenny was pushing them together. Casey forced a smile. Feeling trapped—how could she explain her reluctance to attend without sounding like a complete idiot or without lying—she said, "I—well, I don't think I have anything planned."

"Good," Jenny said, as she slipped her arm through her husband's, looking pleased with herself. "We really should get home to the kids."

Pastor Ed patted his wife's hand and smiled lovingly down at her. "Yes, we should." To Jake and Casey he said, "Looking forward to seeing you both tomorrow. Good night." The pair walked over to a sedan parked at the curb, got in and then drove away.

"I better get back to your sister and my daughter," Jake said. "Walk back with me?"

"I really need to get home," she said, desperate to have some time alone to process what had just happened. Was she actually going to go on a date with Jake? Her pulse sped up.

Jake captured her hand. Warmth from his palm sent shivers of awareness up her arm, to curl around her heart, soothing the scars left by another.

*Oh, boy.* What was she getting herself into?

"What time tomorrow should we meet at The General Store?" he asked.

"Ten?"

He gave her hand a squeeze before letting go. "Perfect. We'll see you then."

Casey nodded and watched him walk back down the street toward Lizbet's. How had her life careened out of control? First, Jake enters her life, requesting a tour and help shopping. Then her sister shows up unannounced, invading her life. And now Casey had been roped into going with Jake to a singles group church social.

Her head was spinning. And she feared protecting her heart was about to get harder than ever.

## Chapter Four

Saturday morning, Casey awoke, ran ten miles, showered and dressed. Then she ate a plate of scrambled eggs and made a pot of coffee, all before Amelia staggered out of her bedroom and joined her on the back porch.

The spectacular view of the Canadian Rockies rising out of the earth like majestic beacons of hope always brought peace to Casey's soul. Amy would say that peace came from God. Maybe because God created the beauty of the mountains. But Casey wasn't so sure her own peace came from God or His creations. In those mountains she found solace. First as a child dealing with the loss of her parents, then after Patrick passed on. And even when Amelia left, Casey had headed into the wild, where grief had no place.

Unwanted emotions rose, tightening her chest. She refused to look at them. Instead, she forced them down as she always did. The urge to go for a long hike made her hands flex in a fierce grip around the mug in her hands.

"There's coffee made," Casey said, as Amelia plopped in the chair beside her.

Amelia grunted and pulled the hood of her sweatshirt farther over her head. She reminded Casey of a turtle tucking inside its shell. "What time it is?" Amelia asked.

Casey glanced at her watch. "A little before nine."

"Why are you up so early?"

Casey chuckled. "Still more a night owl than a morning person, huh?"

"Not anymore. I'm at the store by seven," Amelia answered, with a slight defensive note in her voice.

Slanting Amelia a quick glance, Casey said, "You haven't been sleeping very well. I heard you moving around during the night several times. What's up?"

"Nothing. I just don't sleep well."

Casey didn't believe her. She knew what she'd heard, and the dark circles under Amelia's eyes told the real story. "Anything you want to talk about? I'm a good listener."

"Good to know." Amelia pushed herself up from the chair. "Time to get ready. We're meeting Jake and Veronica at The General Store at ten."

Casey choked on her coffee. *He'd invited Amelia?* Why did that sting?

"You okay?"

Able to breathe again, Casey, said, "Yes. Just went down the wrong pipe."

It made sense he'd ask Amelia to join them, because she'd need to be outfitted, as well. And hadn't she already decided that Jake inviting her to shop with him and his daughter was all business and not personal? But still…the sting tightened in her chest, creating a fiery ache. "I suppose he mentioned the church barbeque, too."

"No, but I love a good barbeque," Amelia said. "Oh, no. You have coffee all over your shirt. Rinse it with cold water. Do you have stain remover?"

*Great.* Casey stared down at the brown spots dotting the cream-colored turtleneck she wore. It was going to be one of those of days.

The phone in the house rang.

"Would you mind getting that while I change my shirt?" Casey asked.

Amelia didn't move. "Anyone I know would call me on my cell."

"Right." Like that explained her unwillingness to help out. With a sigh of resignation, Casey stood and went inside. She checked the caller ID and didn't recognize the number. "Hello?"

"Is this Casey?" asked a deep voice that sent her heart thumping.

"Jake?"

"Yes. Hi, I'm sorry to bother you at home. Reed gave me your number. He got it from Amy."

Surprised pleasure infused her. "No one has gone through so much effort to talk to me." She laughed, then her cheeks heated when she realized how lame she sounded. "What can I do for you?"

"I needed to let you know we've had a change in plans," he said.

Yep, one of those days. Disappointment spiraled to her toes, though on some level she wasn't truly surprised. Jake and his daughter weren't the outdoorsy type. A lot of people backed out of their scheduled tours once they realized the enormity of the trip. "Okay, I understand. I'm sure Amy will refund your deposit."

"What? Oh, no. We're still going on the tour, it's just my parents have decided they'd like to leave this morning for Juneau, rather than tomorrow. Veronica and I are driving them down. I have the list of supplies. We'll pick up everything we need in Juneau."

"Oh." Oh! He was calling to cancel the shopping. And the church barbeque. She was relieved about the latter. Dating was such a nerve-racking experience. And the thought of where a date might lead made her palms sweat. Better to not go down that road.

"Great. Make sure you both wear your hiking boots on your trip back. That will help to break them in," she advised.

"Will do. See you Monday morning. Bye."

"Bye."

Casey hung up the phone and turned to find Amelia watching her from the doorway. "That was Jake. He and Veronica are driving his parents to Juneau this morning."

Amelia's mouth turned down in a pout. "I'm going back to bed."

"What about shopping for you?" Casey said.

Amelia waved a hand. "I already ordered several things online last night. I paid extra for rushing shipping. They should arrive this afternoon."

Casey shook her head as Amelia glided from the room. This next week was going to be very interesting, indeed.


Monday morning, before heading out of her house for the tour company offices, Casey knocked on Amelia's door.

"What?!"

Casey cracked the door open and peered in. Amelia had never been a good morning person, and Casey knew from experience how testy she could be, kind of like poking a bear in its den. Amelia lay on her side, the covers tucked up to her chin and a bright pink eye mask covering the top half of her face. "Hey, I'm heading on over to the tour company. You probably might want to start getting ready."

"I will," came the grumbled reply, as Amelia turned over, giving Casey her back.

Wondering if she should set Amelia's alarm, Casey glanced around the room. Pepto Bismol–pink walls and lots of frills, just as it had been when Amelia was a kid. Casey had kept Amelia's things in place after Amelia left town. The vanity, with all the little light bulbs outlining the mirror, and the puffy pink stool were covered with discarded clothes.

Mostly Amelia's purchases from the Internet. Fancy clothes at a fancy price. A pair of brown hiking boots were still in the box. No matter how much Casey had encouraged Amelia to wear them for a while over the weekend, Amelia refused. Casey made a mental note to pack extra moleskin for blisters.

"You can park your rental in the employee parking lot, not out on the street, okay?"

"Yeah," came the muffled reply.

"You have an hour," Casey said, as she shut the door, unwilling to be her sister's keeper.

Having already loaded her pack and additional supplies in her Jeep, Casey drove to the office. She noted several cars already parked in the employee-designated area. Some she recognized as those of a few of the other tour guides, the rest she guessed belonged to her clients. Were Jake and Veronica already here?

A little spurt of excitement, mixed with a dose of anxiety, shot through her veins.

*Oh, get a grip,* she chided herself. *Jake is just a client. Nothing more.*

He was way to citified for her tastes. Really, she should be more worried about the photographer. Though he said he was hoping to capture the real Alaska on this tour, to sell to an outdoor magazine, unease slithered in her belly. Stan could reinforce the whole "she's just one of the guys" image with unflattering photos.

When she entered the offices through the employee side entrance, Rachel called out to her.

"Casey, Amy wants to see you in her office."

Casey smiled her thanks and bypassed the large space that housed the many tour guides' cubicles, and headed down the hall toward Amy's private office. She knocked before opening the door.

Amy sat at her desk, intently studying the

yellowed parchment spread over the desktop. Her red hair was pulled away from her face and held at the nape of her neck by a clip. She glanced up and smiled. "Come here. Shut the door behind you."

Complying, Casey moved to stand beside Amy's chair. "Is this the map everyone's been talking about?"

Amy grimaced. "Yes and no. This is the real map. There's a fake one circulating and causing all sorts of trouble. Search-and-rescue has had to go out on numerous occasions to bring back some lost soul prowling the wilds for treasure."

Surprise raised Casey's eyebrows. "So there really is buried treasure out there?"

"Looks like."

"Where did you find the map?"

"The boys did. They were snooping around the kitchen, looking for my cookie hiding place, when they stumbled across a secret door in one of the cupboards."

"Wow. Amy, that is so cool. If you find it, you and the boys would be set for life!"

Amy sat back and shook her head. "No. If the treasure is found, I want the money to go to the town coffers."

That was so like Amy. "Very unselfish and honorable of you."

"No, it's self-serving," she said. "I love this company, but we're struggling. And I love Treasure Creek, but it's going under. That's why I wrote a letter to the outdoor magazine, hoping to garner some business." She made a face. "I hadn't figured my letter would end up on the desk of an editor at *Now Woman* magazine."

"That article has brought a lot of business to town. Surely that's made a difference," Casey said. "The town's been jam-packed with tourists, and we've been booking tours right and left. I even have a freelance photojournalist coming with us, who wants to capture the real Alaska on film. That has to be good for the town."

Amy inclined her head. "The money from the tourist trade has kept us all afloat, but there's no guarantee the dollars rolling in now will be sustained over time. The town council is even contemplating closing the library. And if things get any worse, Treasure Creek could lose its charter." Amy straightened, and a determination tightened her jaw. "I can't let that happen. My great-great-grandfather founded this town. This company was the brainchild of your uncle and Ben. I owe it to them all to make sure we stay solvent."

"That's a lot of responsibility to carry, Amy. And I'm not sure it's all yours."

"Well, that's where you come in," Amy said, with a gleam in her eyes.

Glad to have an opportunity to help her friend, she said, "Tell me how I can help."

Amy sat forward and ran her finger over the map, tracing the path to the spot marked with an *X*. "I want you to take a copy of this map with you on your tour and see if you can find this place."

Casey stared at the parchment. "So this is somewhere between the Chilkoot Trail and the Taiya River."

"Yes. Somewhere in this strip of land is the treasure."

"Would have been nice if your great-great-grandfather would have been a bit more precise. I mean, this X encompasses a huge stretch of terrain."

"As Pastor Michaels would say, 'God never promised life would be easy, only that He'd be with us.'"

The words meant to encourage only stirred

old anger in Casey. Not that she wanted life to be easy per se, but she wanted God to keep His promise. Hadn't the Bible said God would heal the sick? Heal the broken heart? Casey had believed those promises, only to be disappointed.

"I'm sorry, Casey. If you don't want to do this, I understand," Amy said, her gaze searching Casey's face.

Casey hadn't meant for her thoughts to be so visible. "It's not that. I want to help. Of course I'll take the copy of the map and see if I can find the treasure, or at the very least, mark off where it's not."

"Okay, if you're sure." Amy rolled the parchment up and secured it with a ribbon before handing it to Casey. "Be careful. There are some unscrupulous people around town who would love to get their hands on this map. And the treasure."

"I'll guard it well," Casey promised.

And Casey was a woman who kept her promises.

Jake parked his rig near the rear of the parking lot adjacent to the tour company offices. Beside him in the passenger seat, Veronica leaned against the door with her eyes closed. She'd grumbled about getting up and getting ready. He didn't blame her. They'd been late in arriving home last night, after spending the day shopping in Juneau. She'd dragged him from one store to another with vigor worthy of the Energizer Bunny. Now she was moving more at the pace of a slug.

"Come on, sleepyhead," Jake said, touching her arm. "We're here."

Veronica groaned. "Do we have to go?"

For the umpteenth time, Jake answered, "Yes. We do. Come on, just give the tour a chance. You might actually enjoy the outdoors."

Veronica snorted as she opened the door, and climbed out to lean against the side of the vehicle. She wore one of the new outfits they'd purchased. A hundred-plus-dollar pair of pants, made from the latest in hiking material. Thankfully, they'd found a store that specialized in wicking undergarments that had a variety of colors. And yet another store for the most fashionable and functional tops, even some with a screened-on designs. The one she wore now had a burst of flowers covering the front, while the body of the shirt was a pale green.

Finding hiking boots that Veronica would wear had been an ordeal. Jake had found himself wishing fervently that he'd invited Casey to come to Juneau with them, so she could have helped with the shopping exercise. Veronica had finally settled for a pair of boots in a pale blue color that the sales clerk had assured them was the best. *They ought to be, for what they cost,* Jake thought, as he moved around to the back of the four-wheel drive and lifted the hatch.

"Grab your pack," he instructed Veronica.

In a huff, she pushed away from the car and shimmied on one of the two backpacks lying in the trunk.

Jake hoped they'd bought the appropriate type. The packs were top loaders, with a few side pockets and comfy, foam padding on the back. Their tent and sleeping bags were attached with Velcro straps.

Jake hefted his pack onto his back, grabbed his parka and shut the door. "You have your jacket?"

Veronica rolled her eyes. "Yeah. It's tucked inside the pack."

Not wanting to start the day with a confrontation, Jake ignored Veronica's eye rolling. "Come on, then."

He led the way to the tour company. When they entered the building, they found the Caruthers and Stan Ford waiting in the reception area, their packs propped up against the wall. After greeting them, Jake asked the receptionist, "Does Casey know we're here?"

The woman behind the desk smiled, showing off her white teeth. "Yes. She'll be out in a moment."

Anticipation arced through him. But was the sudden, nervous stampede of elephants tromping through his stomach from the knowledge that soon they'd be setting out on their tour? Or was this antsy feeling more related to seeing the tour guide, Casey?

He dismissed the latter and decided he was excited about the trip, because Casey was so not his type. He liked women to look like women. Soft, feminine and playing up their assets.

An image of Casey rose in his mind, dispelling any notion that she was anything less than all-woman, with her rounded curves visible beneath her formfitting unisex shirt and snug cargo pants. His blood pounded in his veins and mocked his resistance to admitting Casey was an attractive woman.

Still, she wasn't the type to want hearth and home. Which, if he ever went down the marriage route again, was what he'd want. Someone who would be a good mother for his child.

He glanced over at his daughter and sent up a silent prayer that he wasn't making a mistake by insisting she come on this trip. He really wanted Veronica to enjoy the world beyond her magazines and electronics.

Casey stepped into the room. The visceral reaction tightening Jake's gut surprised him. There was just something about her that called out to him. Which was odd, considering she wasn't anything like the sort of woman he usually found attractive.

Her short brown hair was tied back with a band, her creamy complexion was devoid of makeup and her outfit—well-worn cargo pants, a plain, blue thermal shirt peeking out beneath a dark Gortex jacket and her old worn boots—should have been a turnoff. So, what had his pulse jumping and his senses coming to alert mode?

Maybe it was the way her velvety skin beckoned for his touch, the way the blue of her shirt brought out the sparkle in her amazing eyes, or the figure he'd already acknowledged as attention grabbing. His gaze lingered on her lips. Soft, moist and oh, so appealing. Oh, man, wanting to kiss the tour guide was so not the way to start out the week.

Her gaze scanned the room before a little frown appeared. "We'll get started in just a moment. I just need to check on one thing," Casey said, before darting back the way she'd come.

*One thing, meaning her sister,* Jake thought.

A few moments later, the front door to the tour company opened and Amelia Donner walked in, looking like she was ready for a photo shoot for a sports ad campaign, rather than being about to go on a seven-day backpacking trip. Her makeup was skillfully done and her chin-length hair, softly curled at the ends, swung as she walked. She wore snug-fitting stretchy pants, spiffy clean boots, much like the ones Jake had bought, and a soft-looking, long-sleeve shirt that Jake guessed was made from the same type of wicking material he'd purchased for himself and Veronica.

All was appropriate for their hike, but it was the accessories that added flare. Her new boots sported little gold charms dangling from the laces, gold bracelets jangled merrily from her wrists and her backpack was a bright orange color that nearly matched the color of her top and sported a little bling, as well.

All in all, Amelia was a pretty package. But she did nothing for him. Odd.

Her ruby-red lips spread into a smile as her blue gaze swept the room. "Hello, everyone."

Murmurs of "hello" greeted her. Stan, the photographer, lifted his camera. Amelia didn't miss a beat as she paused to pose for the shot. Obviously, Amelia was used to being the center of attention. Most women like her were. That had never bothered Jake before. Natalie had been the same way. Come to think of it, so had most of the women he'd dated over the years. What did that say about him? He didn't want to think of the possible answers.

Man, there he went again with the self-evaluation. Unsettled with his thoughts, Jake picked up a magazine on hiking and stared at the pictures.

"Amelia, come sit here," Veronica said, patting the seat beside her.

After depositing her pack next to the others, Amelia sat next to Veronica.

"Oooh, I love these," Veronica cooed, touching the charms on Amelia's boots.

"Aren't they fun?" Amelia said, wiggling her boot.

Casey reentered the reception room, followed by a tall, muscular man wearing a Stetson, Wrangler jeans and cowboy boots. His green eyes were amused and a smiled tipped the corners of his mouth. He stopped next to Casey and laid a hand on her shoulder, bent close and murmured something in her ear. Suppressed laughter danced in her eyes, but she kept her expression even as she met Jake's gaze.

Jake frowned as a shaft of irritation stabbed through him, unnerving him. *What was that about?*

And why did he care?

"Okay, now that everyone is here," Casey said, with a meaningful glance at her sister. "We can get this party going. But first, I need you all to bring your packs into the prep room where we'll distribute the food and cooking supplies."

Amelia rose and sidled up to Casey. "I remember this yummy man, but not his name."

Addressing the group at large, Casey said, "This is Nate McMann, another one of Alaska's Treasures' tour guides. He'll be driving our shuttle to where we'll pick up the trailhead."

Relief that the cowboy wasn't coming on their trek washed over Jake as he picked up his and Veronica's packs and followed the others out of the room. Why it would matter he didn't know and really didn't want to examine.

"Nice to see you, Nate," Amelia purred, and actually batted her lashes as she held out her hand. "Too bad you're not coming with us."

Jake bit back a laugh. The woman wasn't too subtle.

"Amelia." The big cowboy gave her hand a quick shake and then stepped back. "Oh, you'll be well taken care of with your sister. She's one of the best."

"Hi, Nate," the Caruthers said, in unison, as they moved to pick up their packs.

Stan lifted his chin in greeting as he hefted his pack and trudged out of the room.

Jake picked up his and Veronica's packs and filed out of the reception room behind the others.

In the prep room they found stacks of freeze-dried food packages and cooking utensils near a scale. One by one, Casey and Nate weighed each pack before adding supplies to them.

"One more thing," Casey said, handing out small whistles attached to lanyards. "These are in case you get separated from the group."

Stan tested the small cylindrical instrument with a quick blast that stung Jake's ears. There would be no mistaking that noise.

When the supplies had been distributed, they headed out a back door to the waiting twelve-passenger van. The cowboy drove them out of town a few miles, down a country road, before stopping at a turnout. They piled out of the van.

A simple wooden sign marked the Chilkoot trailhead. Beyond the sign, an old-growth temperate rain forest awaited them. The rushing sound of the Taiya River, the sudden squawk of a bird and the earthy scent of the land made Jake feel alive, yet there was a certain gravity to knowing they were about to embark on a trip once made by those on a quest for gold— many of whom never made it back.

"This is your last chance to use the facilities," Casey said, and pointed to the crude restrooms.

All the women dropped their packs and headed off. Only Casey remained behind.

"How many times have you made this trek?" Jake asked, as he came to stand beside her, the clean, citrusy scent of her hair teasing his nose, sending a sudden, powerful desire to lean closer and breathe deep arcing through him.

"Hard to say." She adjusted her pack and secured the small shovel on the side with a Velcro strap. "I make it at least once a month, except during winter." She gave him a searching look. "There's still time to back out, you know."

He shook his head, hating that she had doubts about his stamina. He'd grown up in Treasure Creek, though admittedly, he'd never taken advantage of the outdoors like he could have. His mistake—not one he was going to repeat, now that he was back in town for good. He'd show her he wasn't some sissy city boy. "No. We're doing this."

Her pleased smile zinged straight to his heart.

## Chapter Five

When everyone had regrouped, they set off in single file with Casey in the lead. The Caruthers and Stan peppered Casey with questions while Amelia and Veronica brought up the rear. Jake was sandwiched between. He paid attention to Casey's melodic voice while also keeping an eye on his daughter. He already anticipated the crick he'd have in his neck by the end of the day.

The ground was level for a while, and Jake found himself fascinated with the beauty of the forest. Every time he pointed out something interesting in the foliage to Veronica, like the plants with the leaves as big as plates or the spidery ferns, she'd give a long-suffering sigh and nod. He wanted to give up after a while, but he knew he shouldn't. At some point, she had to become interested, didn't she?

The terrain changed as they gradually began to climb over a set of stair steps made of rocks and roots. Water bubbled up from the ground, pooling in spots. Jake's legs and feet were starting to feel the burn—as were his daughter's, as she loudly made sure everyone knew. They stopped for lunch near an old boiler that had been left to rust.

"This was used to generate electricity for the tramways, back when the gold rush was in its heyday," Casey explained.

"Not very eco-friendly to leave it out here," Stan stated, as he snapped off shots.

"You'll see all sorts of paraphernalia left by the miners along the trail," Casey said. "The Chilkoot Trail is considered the world's longest museum by some."

"Goody. Just what I want to see. Old rusty stuff," Veronica said.

Casey smiled at the girl. "I felt that same way when I was your age. But now I realize how much history has been left behind."

"Whatever," Veronica intoned, in a bored voice.

"Veronica," Jake cautioned. He had a bad feeling in the pit of his stomach. This was going to be a long week.

Casey was glad to see the warm-up shelter of the Finnegan's Point campsite appear in the dense forest. She was also glad no other campers were using the area, though she knew some could arrive at any time. But this way, her tour got the pick of the best spot.

It had been a long day, with the constant complaining of Jake's daughter. Surprisingly, Amelia hadn't said much about feeling fatigued, though Casey had noticed she'd kept up a running dialogue with Jake, asking him all kinds of questions about his business and his life. Casey had tried not to listen, but couldn't help hearing a few tidbits. His father was retiring; he still owned his home in Chicago; and he had plans to take Veronica to Hawaii for spring break. Casey could just imagine Amelia salivating to go on that trip.

"Here we are," Casey said, as she halted in the spot where she liked to camp. The roomy space between the tall spruce and aspen trees provided a canopy from any rain with their branches, and was the flattest in the area. "Pick a spot and pitch your tent. We'll be eating in the warm-up shelter and poling everything else."

"Poling?" Marie Caruthers asked.

"See those tall poles sticking out of the ground?" She pointed about twenty yards away, between some more trees, where four poles rose out of the ground about fifteen feet high. Wooden branches had been tied cross-wise to make an arbor of sorts. "We'll hoist all the food, and anything else that has a scent and that you don't need in the tent with you at night, up on those poles."

Amelia's gaze went from the poles to Casey. "Why?"

Casey knew it was best to just get this over with.

"Bears."

Amelia's gaze widened. Veronica stepped closer to her father. The Caruthers looked at each other. Only Stan seemed pleased by the prospect.

"Cool. I hope I can capture a shot of a bear. What kind?" he asked.

"Mostly black bears and grizzlies. But

they've grown used to having humans in their territory."

"I've read that bears don't usually venture near hikers unless they leave food out," Maria Caruthers said, in a soothing, motherly tone. "Which I'm sure we won't."

Grateful to the older woman for her support, Casey said, "That is correct."

"So my cherry-flavored lip gloss needs to go up there?" Veronica asked.

"I'm afraid so," Casey replied, and cut a glance toward the kid, expecting to see sarcasm or disdain on her fine features. But the vulnerability and the trace of fear in her wide eyes reminded Casey that behind the surly attitude and grumbling, Veronica Rodgers was still only a twelve-year-old girl. Compassion filled Casey. She remembered all too well what it was like growing up without a mother. And to be out in the wilds, when Veronica was used to the city, well, that had to be a tad scary.

Offering Veronica a gentle smile, Casey said, "We just need to be cautious. It's highly unlikely a bear will bother us."

"But we *are* in their space, right?" Amelia asked, her alert gaze canvassing the woods.

"So really, we aren't that safe out here, are we?"

Needing to reassure everyone, Casey said, "We are safe. But we still need to be cautious." Hoping to distract her travelers, she continued, "Now, let's set up our tents, then we can head to the warm-up cabin for dinner."

The task of pitching tents took way longer than Casey anticipated. Amelia was useless as Casey pitched the tent they would share. Stan had trouble untangling his cables, but with some help from Jake managed to get it done. The Caruthers put theirs up inside out and had to redo it. And the methodical way Jake went about setting up his tent was both fascinating and curious. Did he approach everything in his life in so orderly a manner?

The sun hung low in the sky, as close to setting as it came this time of the year in this part of Alaska, by the time they made the short trek to the warm-up cabin where Casey, with Jake's help, built a fire. Maria and her husband set out food as Casey set water to boil for rehydrating the freeze-dried meals.

"Really? Pot roast and potatoes au gratin?" Amelia asked, inspecting the packages.

"Don't forget the green beans," Stan

quipped, as he came to stand beside Amelia, his gaze adoring.

"Right." She shivered. "I'm going back inside where it's warm. Call me when dinner's ready."

Stan followed her inside like a puppy.

"Is this hard for you? Having your sister along?" Jake asked quietly as he took a seat next to Casey on a log.

Casey thought about the question for a moment. "I wouldn't say 'hard.' Yet. But this is only day one of six."

"True. I'm hoping Veronica will last. She's already in her sleeping bag."

"That's not unusual for the first day. Make sure she eats plenty in the morning, to keep up her strength."

"Will do."

Casey tended the fire. Her thoughts turned to the map tucked safely in her backpack. Tomorrow they would enter the area along the river where she would poke around, searching for the lost treasure. An impossible task, given that the map was so vague. There were hundreds of miles to cover between the Chilkoot Trail and the river, with the only significant landmark on the map an outcropping along the riverbank.

A coal sparked, sending a stray ember to land near her feet. Jake shifted and their legs brushed, as he used the toe of his boot to stomp out the piece of glowing coal.

Shivers of awareness ran a marathon over Casey. A pleasant sensation. "Thanks," she murmured.

From off to the right of camp a twig snapped.

Marie froze in the act of setting out plates. "Could that be a bear?"

Doug moved protectively to her side.

Jake stood, as if prepared to take on an animal. Pure he-man and admirable.

Casey remained seated. "Bears aren't usually so bold as to venture near camp while we're around. Maybe an ermine or fox," she said. "Or more hikers coming in."

Jake sat back down and the Caruthers seemed to relax, but Marie kept glancing over her shoulder before she and Doug entered the warm-up shelter. Casey understood her nervousness. If someone wasn't used to the wilderness, it could be frightening.

Jake remained quiet for a moment before

asking, "So what's the story with you and the cowboy?"

A surprised laugh escaped Casey. Talk about out of the blue. "Me and...Nate? We're coworkers. Friends."

His tense jaw relaxed. "Good."

She arched an eyebrow at him, hoping he'd explain why that was good. He sounded like he was jealous. But that couldn't be. Could it?

Instead, he said, "The water's boiling. I'll let everyone know it's time to eat."

He rose and hurried into the shelter.

Casey pondered the exchange. Curiosity as to why he would ask such a question burned in her belly. Possible answers that came to mind sent intriguing thrills up her spine.

Could Jake be interested in her? If so, how did she feel about it?

She honestly didn't know.

The next day proved to be a bit more rigorous for Veronica, and Jake found his patience wearing thin. The terrain made a few steep climbs, giving rare glimpses of the snow-capped mountains above the trees, and then took a steep descent back toward the Taiya riverbank. He'd had to prod her along. They'd been passed by two other hiking groups.

At the suspension bridge that crossed the rushing waters of the river, Veronica balked.

"No way am I going across that," she said. She clung to the side of the rope staked to the ground at the river's edge. Her backpack bowed her shoulders slightly. Today was cooler, and she'd donned her jacket and a knit hat over her strawberry-blond hair. Her blue eyes looked enormous in her pale face, as she stared transfixed at the water.

"Come on, Veronica. It's a piece of cake," Amelia said, and strutted across the wooden slats behind the others. The bridge wobbled slightly but Amelia kept walking until she reached the other side, where the Caruthers and Stan waited.

"Veronica, there's no other way across," Jake said, afraid this might be the point that forced the two of them to turn back.

Casey stepped to Veronica's side. "I know you're scared. And it's okay. We all get scared at times." She put her hand over Veronica's on the rope. "The first time I crossed this bridge I thought for sure I'd fall through or fall off. But I didn't. And neither will you. I promise."

"I'm not going across," Veronica insisted.

Jake met Casey's gaze and gave a helpless gesture. He didn't know how to make his daughter brave enough to cross the bridge, and wasn't sure if he should force her to. Would that traumatize her? Or would it be worse to let her fear win?

"How about this?" Casey said, her voice calm yet firm. "You hold my hand and your dad's hand while we all cross together."

Casey held out her free hand to Jake. He slid his palm over hers, felt the strength in her fingers as she guided his hand to cover his daughter's other hand. Slowly, Veronica released the rope and gripped his hand. With Casey in the lead, they walked single file across the gently rocking bridge. When they reached the other side, Jake hugged Veronica as pride filled him. "You did it."

She clung to him for a moment before pushing away and tramping off behind Amelia and the others. Jake caught Casey's hand as she moved past him. Gratitude and affection filled his heart. "Thank you."

She smiled, her blue eyes tender. "Not a problem."

For a moment they stood still, their hands intertwined while the rush of river water, the scent of earth and trees enveloped them. A curious longing spread through Jake. More than attraction. A deeper need for connection gripped him.

His gaze dropped to Casey's pink lips. Attraction he could deal with, if not totally understand, considering she was nothing like the women who usually drew his attention.

The other part…well, it had to be the fact that she was so good with his daughter. That was all. His daughter meant the world to him, and Casey's kindness to her made her a heroine in his eyes.

He could feel himself leaning slightly toward her, drawn to her in a way he hadn't expected, and helpless to resist.

Her sharp intake of breath jerked his gaze from her mouth.

The expression of surprise, and an answering attraction on her pretty face as she stared into his eyes, had sanity returning in a crashing wave. What was he doing?

He stepped back and released her hand. He

opened his mouth to speak but didn't know what to say, how to explain his behavior. Instead, he said, "We should catch up with the others."

Without waiting for a reply, he walked away, forcing himself to breath deep.

*Get a grip, man.* Even if Casey Donner were his type, he wasn't interested in any kind of relationship right now. His daughter was the priority.

And he would do well to remember that.

Casey stared after Jake, as a mixture of astonishment and irritation cascaded over her like the river rushing over the rocks. Last night he'd acted a bit strange, asking about her relationship with Nate, as if he were scoping out her availability. Today he nearly kissed her—and then backed away, as if he'd realized doing so was a bad idea.

But what really had her bacon frying was the fact that she'd wanted him to kiss her.

She'd been ready to dive headlong into the moment, anticipation stealing her breath and making all the reasons why sharing a kiss with Jake Rodgers would be a bad idea melt away like a snowflake touching down on hot cement.

She should be glad he'd saved them both from the embarrassing aftermath of such an intimacy.

Knowing she should, and actually feeling glad, were two very different things, though. For just once, she wished she could be more like her sister and be casual about life and love. She wasn't. Both were serious subjects.

And no matter how attractive she found Jake, she had to stay professional on this trip. For everyone's sake.

The sudden sensation of being watched slithered across her skin. She glanced around. Across the water she thought she saw movement, the rustle of a bush, the bowing of a tree branch. She listened, but heard only the rhythmic sounds of the flowing water.

Dismissing the impression as antics of her overactive mind, she adjusted her pack and hurried after her group.

They broke for lunch along the sandbar of Pleasant Camp. Casey was careful to keep a distance from Jake. She really wasn't sure how to act, so she settled for pretending nothing happened.

Well, nothing had. Really. She was making too much out of the moment.

She helped Stan and Doug with their folding fishing poles, and set them to trolling the rushing waters for one of the many varieties of salmon or trout that were abundant in the frigid waters.

"We'll rest here for a couple of hours. Feel free to explore the area. But make sure you don't venture too far," she advised the group. "If you search along the river's edge, you might find some interesting rocks. Maybe even some with fossils embedded in them. Also a good time to do a sponge-off."

Leaving the group to their own devices, Casey set off with the map tucked into her jacket. Once out of view of the others, she took it out and studied the crude drawing. Since the outcropping drawn on the map wasn't visible from Pleasant Camp, she headed north along the shore until the land merged with the water and she couldn't go any farther. She kept her eyes peeled for anything that resembled an outcropping formation, but the steep sides of the mountains flanking the river were covered with trees, not boulders. At least she could tell Amy the treasure wasn't north of Pleasant Camp.

Taking advantage of the solitude, she dug out a bar of biodegradable soap from her pack and spent the next half hour sponging off in the frigid waters. When she was done, with her pack secured in place, she retraced her steps.

The strange sensation of being watched that she'd experienced before at the bridge prickled her skin again and taunted her all the way back. Once she'd rejoined the others, she tried to relax and eat, but the thought that something out there was following them put a sense of urgency in her step as she hustled everyone back onto the trail.

They made camp at dusk at a place called Sheep Camp. Jake couldn't fathom the name, since there was no meadow, nor sheep. Just more of the same lush rain forest, a warm-up shelter and bear poles. The temperature had dropped to the thirties and a slight breeze stirred the fresh, pine-scented air.

After pitching his tent, he moved near the fire to watch the dancing flames. Veronica,

Amelia and Stan had moved inside the shelter, while the Caruthers had volunteered to gather more wood for the fire. Casey tended the cooking gear, her gaze never once straying toward him. In fact, ever since their near miss of a kiss, she'd been avoiding talking directly to him, or coming near.

He didn't blame her. He'd acted like a jerk. He should have just said his thank-you and moved on, instead of losing his head to attraction and emotion.

His daughter's giggle drew his attention as she stepped out of the warm-up cabin. Her face was flushed with good health and her smile lit up her face. When she wasn't grumbling, she was actually enjoying herself. Jake's heart squeezed tight with love for this child of his. From the moment he'd held her in his arm in the hospital, he knew his life would never be the same. He would do anything for Veronica.

"Daddy," she said, as she came to sit beside him. "When we get back, Amelia said she'd help me with school clothes shopping. She knows all about fashion and stuff. She even said that the store she works for hires kids as young as sixteen to help stock the clothes.

We should move to San Francisco so I can do that."

Groaning inwardly, Jake tried to keep annoyance from showing on his face. "Honey, my job isn't in San Francisco. Our lives are now here in Treasure Creek."

She sighed. "I knew you'd say no."

"Once school starts and you make some friends, you'll like it here," Jake promised.

Veronica shrugged. "Maybe. But I'm going to go to college to be a fashion designer. Amelia said there are schools specifically for that."

"I'm sure there are." Jake didn't want to point out that college was still six years away and she might change her mind by then.

A shout startled Veronica into a yelp. The sound of someone crashing through the trees had Jake jumping to his feet. Casey's concerned gaze met his over the fire, before she headed in the direction of the noise.

"Hey," Jake said, moving quickly to intercept her. "It might not be safe."

A frown marred her brow. She shook off his hand. "Get your daughter in the shelter and keep the others there."

Not about to let her face danger alone,

Jake swiveled to speak to his daughter. "Go inside."

Veronica scrambled to do as told.

Just then, Marie and Doug Caruthers burst into camp. Marie's eyes were wide with fright. Doug stopped and turned, as if expecting someone to be following them.

"What happened?" Casey asked, taking Marie by the hand and leading her to the log.

Jake moved to Doug's side. "A bear?"

Doug shook his head. "No. It was man. He was watching us. When I shouted to him, he took off running. I thought he was headed here, but obviously not."

A thought slammed into Jake's mind. "It could be Tucker," he said aloud. "What did he look like?"

Doug held up his head to just over his head. "I'd say six feet. I couldn't see his face. He wore a hooded jacket."

Casey moved to his side. "Are you talking about Tucker Lawson? The guy who's plane disappeared?"

"Yes." The torment of remorse for not having been a better friend clawed at his throat. "This isn't anywhere near where they hypothesize his plane went down, but maybe—"

"He was your friend?"

"He *is*." Guilt forged a flowing river in Jake's mind. "Only, I wasn't there for him when he needed me. If I had been, maybe he wouldn't have taken off in that plane."

"You don't honestly feel responsible for his disappearance, do you?"

"I do. And if he's out there I want to find him. I've been funding the local search-and-rescue's efforts. I owe it to Tucker."

She considered him for a moment. "Okay."

"Okay?"

She nodded before hurrying to her tent and disappearing inside. When she returned, she had clipped a hunting knife to her belt and slung a smaller pack over her shoulder. "Let's go."

Admiration for this woman's can-do attitude and courage tore through Jake as they set out into the forest.

They searched, calling Tucker's name, but found nothing. No plane, no sign of anyone else. Tired and discouraged, they headed back to camp.

Disappointment ricocheted inside Jake's chest, making him ache. He stopped Casey a few feet from camp. "Would you mind praying with me for Tucker's safety?"

Casey's eyes widened. "I don't. I mean…I haven't. I am probably not the best person to ask."

"I'm sorry. I just assumed, since you knew Pastor Michaels and his wife so well that you were a churchgoer."

"I do attend on occasion. I just don't feel comfortable praying," she said and side-stepped past him.

"Ever? Or just with me?"

She stopped but didn't turn around. "Both."

There was a world of heartache in the word, and that tore at his heart. He moved to stand beside her, his shoulder touching hers. He felt the little shiver that raced through her and an answering one raced through him. He studied her profile. The straight nose, the high cheekbones, lips pressed tightly together. Her gaze was downcast, showing off the long, sweeping slope of dark lashes. She wore a bright yellow knit beanie, her tufts of dark hair curling over the rim. The creamy expanse of her elegant neck made his mouth go dry. He wanted to press his lips to the soft, tender spot where her pulse beat a rhythmic cadence.

He held himself still. "Why can't you pray?"

"There's no point. God doesn't keep His promises."

Aching for her obvious pain, Jake laid his hand on her shoulder. "What promises?"

"To heal the sick."

The breath squeezed from his lungs. *She's lost someone to illness.* The logical conclusion was her uncle. "How did Patrick die?"

She flinched and a small moan escaped her lips. She shook her head, conveying her unwillingness to say. Jake felt a pulsing in his soul that pushed for him to press her into to talking. He knew keeping the hurt inside served only to eat away at faith, at hope and at love. His pastor back in Chicago had taught him that bringing everything into light cast out the darkness. And he sensed a dark place in Casey that needed God's healing light.

Placing his hand on her shoulder, he drew her to his chest. With gentle, soothing strokes, he ran his hands up and down her arms. "Tell me."

She stiffened against him. "It's too hard to talk about."

"Keeping it inside isn't doing you any good."

"You won't understand."

"Try me." When she remained silent, he said, "How old were you when he passed on?"

"Eighteen."

He could imagine how hard that must have been for her at such a young age. "How long was he sick?"

"A year. For a year I prayed every day that God would heal him. But he just got sicker instead of better. Why would God do that? Why does the Bible say God heals the sick, when He doesn't?" Her voice caught on a sob.

How could He help her understand the mysteries of God when he didn't understand them himself?

*Lord, I need Your words here.*

## *Chapter Six*

With only his faith as his guide, Jake asked, "Casey, do you believe in heaven?"

She sniffed. "Yeah, sure."

"Do you believe that Patrick is there?"

She nodded. "Yes. Patrick had a deep faith. Even at the end, he—" She took a shuddering breath. "He said he would see me again in heaven."

Jake turned her to face him. Her lovely face was streaked with tears, her eyes rimmed red and her lips quivering. He cupped her cheek and used his thumb to wipe a tear. "Yes, God didn't heal Patrick here on earth. But He did heal him in heaven."

"But why did he have to die?"

Jake shook his head. Trite words about it

being Patrick's time came to mind, but he held them in check. Casey deserved more than clichéd phrases that were meant to comfort but made no sense of the situation. "I know you miss him. But being angry at God won't bring him back."

Anger, directed at him, flashed in her blue eyes as she stepped back out of his reach. "I know that."

"Do you? It's been ten years, Casey. Ten years of wallowing in your anger. Don't you think it's time to let go and let God heal your grieving heart?"

She arched an eyebrow. "Is that what you did when your wife died?"

Stunned by how neatly she'd parried his words and turned them back on him, he said, "Not when she died. Before that. When she abandoned Veronica and me."

She blinked as her shoulders sagged and the fight drained out of her. "Then you're a better person than I am." She turned and walked back toward camp.

Jake knew it wasn't a matter of being a better person, but rather a matter of giving up a useless emotion that slowly tried to destroy him.

He could only pray that Casey wouldn't let her anger destroy her.

Casey hadn't felt the least bit sleepy when she'd entered the tent a few hours earlier. So she'd unrolled the map and used her flashlight to study the crude drawing again. Finding no satisfaction in that endeavor, not to mention having no clearer idea of where the treasure could be, she finally tried to calm her mind and lay down. But she tossed and turned, which was a difficult feat inside the narrow confines of her down sleeping bag. Every time she rolled, a blast of cold air swooped in to taunt her desire to sleep. Her restlessness was due to Jake. His words played over in her mind: "Don't you think it's time to let go and let God heal your grieving heart?"

Pastor Michaels had said something similar, something about allowing God to be her comfort rather than her enemy. He'd also said that sickness was a part of life. A part she hated.

Her fists clenched beneath the soft material of her bag. Tears seeped from her closed eyes. A deep welling in her soul made her stomach clench. The need to cry out to God, to ask for what she so desperately craved lay lodged in her throat. Trapped by anger, by fear. Fear that if she let go, she'd forget. The way she'd forgotten her parents.

*Ugh!*

She flipped over, wiggling down to get in a more comfortable position.

A rustling near the door of the tent echoed in her ears. The quiet slide of the zipper teeth giving away to pressure as it opened filled her ears. She froze. Amelia?

Slowly, she inched the edge of the sleeping bag down to peer out. Her sister slept on her back, encased within her mummy bag. Only her face showed, her eye mask securely in place.

Heart pounding against her ribs, Casey curled to the side so that she didn't startle whoever was trying to enter her tent. Maybe Veronica needed something?

The flap of the tent door was pulled aside. An unfamiliar man's face appeared in the opening. Casey reached for her hunting knife tucked beneath her pillow. The man didn't notice her, he was too intent on the rolled map lying in the corner. His arm snaked inside, straining to reach the map where she'd laid it on top of her pack.

Amy's warning about unscrupulous people wanting to get their hands on the map and the treasure flashed through Casey's mind.

"Hey!" Casey shouted and in a swift motion sat up, bringing the knife around in front of her.

The man's startled gaze met hers before he scrambled away and disappeared. Casey untangled herself from her bag and grabbed the map.

"What? What's happening?" Amelia asked, lifting the edge of her mask to blink sleepy eyes at Casey.

"It's okay. Bad dream. Go back to sleep," Casey said, not wanting to deal with an hysterical sister on top of a would-be thief.

Quickly pulling on her boots over her thick woolen socks, Casey cautiously left the tent, holding the knife out in front of her, in case the thief was still about. The chilly air seeped through her base-layer, stretch-jersey pants and long-sleeve shirt.

Her shout had awakened the others. Jake unzipped his tent and came out. He wore warm-looking sweat bottoms and a thermal shirt. The Caruthers peered out of their tent, both wide-eyed with fright.

Stan stumbled out of his tent in flannel drawstring pants and a T-shirt, clutching his camera. "What happened?"

Casey debated her options. Tell the group about the thief and the map, or brush the incident aside? Knowing the safety of the group outweighed the consequences of revealing the map, Casey said, "Someone tried to get into my tent to steal this." She held up the rolled paper. "I scared him off, but I'm not sure he's gone for good."

"The guy we saw earlier," Doug stated, with certainty, as he and Marie emerged from their tent. They wore matching thermal long johns and thick wool socks, making Casey think of Thing 1 and Thing 2 from Dr. Seuss.

"Probably," Casey said. "He must have been watching us. Or me, rather." She tugged on her bottom lip. "I had this out and was looking at it before trying to sleep."

"What is that?" Jake asked, as he came to her side, his face searching hers.

She sighed and hoped Amy would understand. "It's a treasure map."

"I heard about that in town," Stan said, his

gaze excited as he moved closer. "There's supposed to be buried treasure somewhere along the Chilkoot Trail. I just thought it was a myth."

"It is," Jake said, his gaze catching Casey's. "There's a bogus map that someone made up and has been circulating for the past month. Just more PR for the area. Chief Truscott told me about it. Obviously, the guy following us doesn't know about the fake map."

Latching on to Jake's explanation, Casey nodded. "That's right. There *is* a fake map. I don't know why anyone would think I have anything different."

"Bummer," Stan said, disappointment lacing the word.

"But what do we do about the stranger?" Marie asked.

Jake spoke, his voice determined and firm. "We all will be careful and alert. No going off alone."

"That's right. Also, I think we should sleep in shifts," Casey said.

"Good idea," Jake said, a smile of approval on his face. "We can break up the night into three four-hour shifts. Stan, Doug and I will rotate."

As grateful as she was for his help, Casey took issue with being excluded. "We'll do four three-hour shifts."

Jake opened his mouth, probably to protest, but she arched an eyebrow in challenge, and he promptly closed his mouth and nodded agreement.

Taking control of the situation, Casey said, "Since we have another four hours before we need to be up and going, I'll stand watch while the rest of you try to get some more rest. Tomorrow we'll be climbing out of the tree line and crossing into the alpine tundra of the Canadian side of the pass. This will be one of the harder days, as we'll be traversing over rocks known as The Scales."

Doug and Marie didn't need any further urging. They disappeared back inside their tent, the zippering echoing in the night air.

"Are you sure?" Stan asked, his gaze darting around the shadowed forest.

Not certain to what he referred, Casey said, "Yes. We're safe, and you should get some more rest."

He nodded and headed back to his one-man tent.

Once they were alone, Casey said to Jake,

in a low voice, "I didn't realize Reed had told you about the map."

Jake shrugged. "He mentioned that Amy was giving the original to her guides. I figured, when you went off by yourself today you were searching for the treasure," he answered, in an equally low tone.

"I did."

"And?"

"Nothing. At least not north of Pleasant Camp. Amy will be disappointed."

"I wonder how this guy knew you had the original map."

"That's a good question. I didn't think anyone but Amy and I knew I had it."

"Did you get a good look at the guy?"

She nodded. "Didn't recognize him. He was older, sixtyish, unshaven, pale eyes. He wore a hooded jacket and worn Levis. Just like the guy the Caruthers saw."

"I don't like this. Is there any way to let Reed know?"

"I carry a satellite cell. In the morning I can contact the company and get word to Reed."

"Good enough. Why don't you go rest? I'll take this watch."

"The group's safety is my responsibility," Casey said.

"You go on."

The pale glow of the sun lit up his grin. "You're not going to give an inch, are you?"

"No."

"Okay, then. Help me drag that log over here."

Stubborn man. She followed him to the log they'd used earlier in the evening to sit on by the fire. Each grasping an end, they carried and dragged the log closer to the campsite.

"Grab your sleeping bag," Jake instructed, as he ducked into his tent.

Not used to being ordered about, Casey made a face and quietly retrieved her bag.

Jake came out of his tent, shimmied into his bag and sat on the ground, with his back leaning against the log. He patted the space beside him.

Following his lead, she stepped into her bag and then sat with the ends tucked around her shoulders and leaned back. "Won't Veronica be worried when she wakes up to find you gone?"

"All she has to do is open the flap and she'll see me. Besides, she's sleeping so hard I don't think anything short of cold water will rouse her."

"Ah, to be young and carefree," she said, quietly.

Extremely aware of him, Casey tried to relax, but the excitement of the thief and Jake's nearness made her restless. The night sounds, usually so soothing and familiar, took on a sinister echo, as nocturnal animals moved about and birds rustled in the trees. With every little noise she started, jerking her gaze in the direction from which it came.

"Jumpy?"

Ruefully, she nodded. "Yeah. That guy sneaking into camp really unnerved me. This is the first time anything like that has happened while I was leading a tour."

Jake pulled his arm out of his bag and tucked it beneath her bag, to wrap around her shoulders, tugging her closer. Her pulse jumped. Shocked by the gesture, she stiffened, not sure what to think of this turn of events—and even more conflicted about how to feel.

"Come on. Settle back. I'll protect you," he coaxed.

She wasn't sure this city slicker could really do as he promised, but something inside of her longed to believe it—longed to believe in *him*.

Slowly, she calmed her heart rate with a few deep, Pilates-inspired breaths, and allowed herself to sink into him. With his hand, he gave her head a gentle nudge until her cheek rested on the plane between his shoulder and chest. She was surprised to find that, even though they'd been on the trail for two days and had no shower to speak of, he smelled good. A mixture of musky man, earth and the faint trace of woodspice. *He must have taken advantage of the river this afternoon,* she thought, as her eyelids grew heavy. She blinked, trying to fight the sleep and sense of well-being that pulled at her. Somehow, she felt secure in the crook of his arm.

As she drifted off, a strident voice inside her head taunted that this wasn't real, that getting too attached to this man would only bring heartache. Mentally, she shushed the voice and fell asleep.

Jake couldn't believe how right it felt to have Casey tucked against his shoulder, or how protective he felt of her. The thought of someone hurting her made his blood boil. He tried to tell himself he'd feel protective of any woman. But deep inside, in a place he really didn't want to look at too closely, he knew there was something about Casey Donner that got under his skin. It didn't make sense.

He should be attracted to Amelia. She was, after all, polished and sophisticated, and she had made it clear on numerous occasions she was interested in him. Casey, on the other hand…well, her interest didn't much move past the client-customer relationship.

The memory of the look of expectancy and yearning in her eyes when he'd dipped his head to kiss her earlier that day flashed through his mind, making him wonder if this tough and independent woman could find a place in her heart for a guy like him.

Who was he kidding? They were as opposite as night and day, as different as city and country. He could think of a million clichéd phrases to describe their situation. All were accurate, which was why they were clichés to begin with.

And this whole thought process was only an exercise in futility, anyway. *Stay focused,* he reprimanded himself. *Get through this trip. Get back to work. Make sure Veronica gets acclimated to Treasure Creek*. Those were his goals, and Casey Donner did not fit in.

Casey sighed in her sleep and snuggled closer.

His heart squeezed tight. Too bad he wished she did.


Casey clambered up the rocks at the base of the pass, careful not to dislodge any loose debris for the rest of the party behind her. The steep pile of boulders, gravel and shale forged through the glacier as a means to reach the other side was marked with orange poles, pointing out the route to take.

It was the third day of their trip, and Casey could tell her group's stamina was waning. Overhead, storm clouds gathered in the distance, meaning rain would soon descend upon them. Casey pushed the group, hoping to reach Happy Camp before the weather released.

They hadn't seen any sign of their unwanted guest from last night, but Jake wasn't taking any chances. He'd insisted on taking the rear guard, making sure his daughter and Amelia stayed with the rest.

When they reached the snowpacked summit, a wicked wind kicked up. The Canadian flag billowed in the stiff breeze, announcing they were crossing the border into Canada.

They took refuge in the warm-up shelter.

"We'll take a short lunch break," Casey announced.

She took her satellite phone from her pack, gestured to Jake that she was going to make the call to the office and moved far away from where everyone was clustered together for a lunch of protein bars, dried fruit and nuts.

Reception wasn't the best, but she could hear Amy's voice well enough, even if she did sound tinny across the line. Casey quickly filled in Amy on the strange man who'd taken a swipe at getting the map.

"This is my fault. I'm so sorry," Amy said. "I told Reed I'd given you the map and my boys overheard. When I took them to town on Monday they told Harry Peterson at The General Store. I'm not sure who else heard, but you know Harry. As much as I like and respect that man, he has a habit of talking way too loud."

Casey knew all too well how boisterous Harry could be. The proprietor of Treasure Creek's general store had been born and raised in the area, knew everyone and kept an eye on Amy, just as the rest of the residents of Treasure Creek did. Though Casey suspected Harry had deeper feelings for Amy than he let on. "I just thought you should know. Jake thinks you should tell Chief Truscott."

"I will. How's it going?"

"Pretty well. We've reached the summit, though a little later than I'd anticipated."

"And you and Amelia?"

"We really haven't had much time alone." At night, when they were both in the tent, Amelia fell asleep so quickly, with the help of a little prescription sleeping aid, there wasn't time for bonding.

"Jake and his daughter?"

Heat traveled up Casey's neck as memories of waking in Jake's arms assaulted her. Sometime after she'd fallen asleep, he'd shifted her so that she was cradled in his arms. When she opened her eyes hours later, and stared up at his handsome face—his eyes closed, his breathing even—she hadn't wanted to move. But then he'd smiled and cracked one eye open, sending her scrambling away. "He's fine, and Veronica is holding up."

"Fine? That's all I get?"

Casey laughed. "Yes."

Amy scoffed. "For now," she said, making it clear she expected Casey to expound on the topic when she arrived back in town.

"I'll let you know if anything else happens. And if Ranger Simon is in residence, I'll let him know. He can call me if he sees the guy come over the pass behind us."

"Great idea. And tell Simon hello."

"Will do. Bye." Casey pressed End just as Jake walked up. She filled him in on the call.

"Too bad," he said. "Some people will do anything for the mere thought of gold. Let's go see the ranger."

They tredged across the hardpacked snow that hadn't thawed, toward the small cabin tucked back in the shadow of the hillside. As they neared, the sound of music floated on the wind from inside the cabin. Looked like Simon was in residence. Casey knocked. A moment later the door opened. A tall, burly man in his fifties greeted them with a booming hello and a bear hug.

"Miss Casey, so glad to see you. How's that pretty boss of yours?" Simon asked, as he ushered them inside.

"Well, thank you. She said to say hello."

Gesturing to Jake, Casey made the introduction. "This is Jake Rodgers, a native of Treasure Creek."

The men shook hands. "Glad to meet you, son."

"Likewise. This is pretty spectacular up here."

"I like it."

"Do you live here year-round?" Jake asked.

Simon shook his head. "Only during the summer months, when we get lots of tourist forging through."

Casey explained about the man who'd been watching their camp last night.

"After the Tanner treasure, eh?" Simon shook his head. "That old story has been bouncing around these parts for decades." He peered at Casey with curiosity in his light brown eyes. "So Amy really found Mack Tanner's treasure map?"

"Yes, sir. But it's pretty vague as to where the treasure is. Somewhere between the Chilkoot Trail and the river, on our side of the mountain."

"Well, don't you worry, missy. If anyone comes over the pass that resembles the fellow you've described, I'll make sure to keep them busy."

"Thank you, Simon. We appreciate it," Casey said.

When they took their leave, Jake said, "I liked that man. He seems real genuine."

"Simon's the best. He and my uncle were friends." The stab of loss that normally pricked heart her whenever she thought about Uncle Patrick seemed less fierce today. She conjured up his smile in her mind and held on to the memory. "We should head out soon. Try to beat the rain down the mountain."

"You need to eat something," Jake said, and produced a protein bar and trail mix bag from his coat pocket. He held both out to her.

"I have food," she said, not used to having someone taking care of her.

"I know you do. But this is quicker."

Acknowledging the truth in his words, she smiled and took the bar. "Thanks."

"You're welcome." He stuffed the trail mix bag back in his pocket.

She unwrapped the bar and took a bite. Her stomach growled as the food hit bottom. She let out a small moan of pleasure. She was hungrier than she'd thought. She glanced up to see Jake's gaze riveted to her face. There was a look in his dark eyes that she couldn't decipher. Giving him a questioning look, she offered the bar to him. "Do you want some?"

He blinked and swallowed hard. "Uh, no. I, uh, will go make sure the others are ready."

Watching him hustle away, Casey shook her head. The man was so confusing and complicated. Maybe that's what happened to a guy when he migrated to the lower 48. He came back north, sending out mixed messages to mystify unsuspecting females.

Well, she wasn't going to let him bamboozle her with his come-hither looks and sudden backing off. Jake Rodgers was so not the kind of guy for her to pin her future on. Though he came awfully close, much to her chagrin.

## Chapter Seven

Jake awoke the next morning not even remotely rested. Though Doug and Stan had rotated guard duty over the camp, Jake had lain awake listening to the rain hitting the tent and dripping off the side. His mind churned. Was the prowler now in custody, or had he slipped past Simon? Or perhaps, having failed to get the map, had the thief turned back the way he'd come?

As the fourth day of their journey unfolded, Jake decided this was the most scenic thus far. Now, as the trail wound around several lakes, the day warmed up and the sun glinted off the water, post-card perfect. They stopped in a clearing near Morrow Lake for lunch. Doug and Marie were already down at the shore with their poles and their food. Needing some distance from the all-too-alluring Casey, Jake decided to try some fishing, as well.

"I'll go with you," Amelia said, when she heard him tell Veronica his plan.

Surprised by her desire to fish, he shrugged. "That's fine." He turned to Veronica. "Do you want to come?"

She wrinkled her nose. "Yuck."

Jake laughed. "You didn't seem to mind eating the salmon the other night."

"Because it was cooked," she said, in a tone that suggested he was an imbecile for not knowing that.

He wasn't going to push her to join him. The phrase *pick your battles* came to mind. "So what are you going to do?"

She rolled her eyes. "Sit here being bored."

Jake glanced at Casey, who'd plopped down on the ground and leaned back against her backpack. Her mouth twisted in an amused smile. He didn't find his daughter's rudeness amusing, but he didn't think chastising her in public was the right thing to do. He blew out a frustrated breath.

"I have an idea for you," Amelia interjected,

and dug through her backpack. She pulled out a small, colorful zipped bag. "Why don't you give my sister a makeover?"

Casey jerked upright. "You brought your makeup bag?"

Amelia gave her a derisive look. "Of course. Do you think I look this good every day naturally?"

Stan snickered.

Veronica leaped on the idea. "Can I, Casey?"

Looking a bit trapped, she blinked up at Veronica.

"Honey, leave Casey alone. She doesn't wear that stuff," Jake said, hoping to save Casey from having to say no.

"She's a girl," Veronica countered. "All girls need to *wear this stuff.*"

"Casey doesn't mind, do you?" Amelia pressed on, with a look at her sister that was a clear attempt to convey she'd better say yes.

"That—" Jake started, only to be stopped by Casey's raised hand.

"It's fine. You and Amelia go fish. Veronica and I will play with the makeup," Casey said, her blue eyes so earnest as she stared at him.

"You're sure?" As much as he wanted

Veronica to connect with and be influenced by Casey's down-to-earth, confident demeanor, he didn't want his daughter to be a pest, either.

Casey waved her hand. "Go."

Amelia tucked her arm through Jake's. "They're fine. Teach me how to fish."

Feeling crowded with Amelia hanging on him, Jake tried not to grimace as he threw one last, questioning glance at Casey. She shooed him away and turned to Veronica, already busy digging into the bag and pulling out all sorts of paraphernalia.

Figuring there wasn't much harm Veronica could do to Casey except annoy her, Jake turned away and escorted Amelia to the lake's shore.

Casey's skin itched as Veronica leaned in close to brush blush across her cheeks. Is this how Amelia's face felt all the time? Trying to keep her mind off the unfamiliar sensations of eye shadow, eyeliner and lipstick, Casey attempted to keep a conversation going with the young girl.

"Do you enjoy math or reading? Science?"

Veronica used her finger to smooth what

she'd just done on Casey's cheek. "Math is easy but boring. Science is boring. I like to read, but I hate English. All that grammar stuff is just yuck. Who cares what a predicate is, or a subjective noun?" Picking up a compact powder case, Veronica continued, "I'm going to be a fashion designer. I don't need to know regular school stuff."

Not wanting to argue over the value of English grammar, Casey said, "I always liked art class. Not the drawing part so much, but the craft part."

Veronica made a face while she dug through the cosmetic bag. "Crafts are for babies."

"What are your favorite subjects in school?" Casey asked.

"I don't like school."

*Should have seen that one coming. Okay. Moving on...* Since Casey's fashion knowledge didn't extend beyond good outdoor wear, she searched for something else to discuss. "What types of books do you read?"

"Not books. Magazines."

"Do you play any sports?"

Veronica scoffed as she brought out a small, bristled brush and gestured with it. "I'm an artist. I don't do sports."

Surely there had to be some topic they could converse on.

"Do you have a pet?"

"No."

"Why not?"

"Close your eyes," Veronica instructed.

Casey complied and felt the not-so-soft touch of the brush's bristles sliding over her face. Now she really felt cakey. She interlaced her fingers to prevent herself from reaching up to scratch at Veronica's handiwork. "You didn't answer my question."

"Dad said animals are too much responsibility."

Interesting. She wouldn't have expected that sort of attitude from Jake. But then again, she hardly knew the man. "What are your favorite movies?"

Veronica pulled back to study Casey's face. She scrunched up her nose. "I didn't get the eyeliner even."

"I'm sure it's fine," Casey said, ready for her to be done.

"Let me fix it." Veronica uncapped the thick black pencil and came at her.

Closing her eyes again, Casey endured the slight pulling of the colored stick gliding

along the edge of her lashes. She heard someone approach and then a soft male chuckle.
Her lids flew open.

Stan grinned at her and raised his camera
to snap off a shot.

Not sure if his mirth was a good thing or
not, Casey held up her hand, stopping Veronica from putting anything more on her face.
"That's enough."

Tucking her long, strawberry-blond hair
under her knit cap, Veronica stood and smiled.
"Pretty."

Casey smiled back, feeling a bit silly by
the amount of pleasure she felt at the girl's
pronouncement. "Is there a mirror?"

Veronica snatched up the cosmetic bag and
rummaged around. "I'll see."

Casey's gaze moved past Veronica, to the
lake, and saw Jake and Amelia were heading back. Feeling the urgency to see her face
before the two arrived, Casey rose. "Let me
find one."

Veronica danced back. "I'm doing it."

Stan held out his camera. "Look here," he
said, indicating the LCD screen on the back.

Casey took one look at herself in the small
square screen and her stomach dropped. A

heated flush spread up her neck. Thick black outlined her eyes. Bright purple eye shadow covered her lids from the lashes to the eyebrows. Pink slashes covered her cheeks. And over it all was a layer of matte powder that tinged her skin a slightly yellow color. To top off the effect were red lips. Unfortunately, the lipstick hadn't exactly stayed within her lip line, making her lips look fat and misshapen.

"Veronica, what did you do?"

Jake's near-shouted question, full of anger and horror, shuddered through Casey. Tears of humiliation sprang to her eyes, but the need to protect the child had her holding up her hand. "She was just playing."

"She made you look like a clown," he said, clearly upset with them both.

Veronica's lip trembled and hurt welled in her eyes. "But they do up the girls on *America's Next Top Model* like that all the time."

Jake let out a snort and took his daughter by the hand, and led her away.

Amelia's giggle was more than Casey could take. She grabbed her backpack and stomped down to the water's edge. On her knees, she dug through her pack and brought out her bar of biodegradable soap and a small towel. She lathered the soap in the water and then scrubbed at her face.

"Hey, that's not going to work," Amelia said, as she knelt down beside Casey and reached for her hands. "Let me do it."

Casey shook her head and batted away Amelia's attempt to help. "Go away. That was so humiliating."

"Oh, come on. The kid was just being a brat. Don't let her get to you." Amelia unscrewed a small bottle of blue liquid and dabbed some on a cotton ball. "Here. This will get the liner off."

Taking the cotton ball, Casey used it to wipe at her eyes. The sudsy liquid felt gentle compared to the harsher soap. Distrust swelled, making suspicions rise. "Did you put her up to that?"

Amelia tsked. "No, of course not."

Not sure she believed her, since this incident smacked of pranks Amelia had pulled when they were children, Casey didn't comment further as she rinsed her face in the chilly lake water and then dried off. "Is the gunk gone?"

"Yes. Back to being you," Amelia stated,

with a grin. "Though you know, if you ever want, I'd be happy to do your makeup right. You could use a touch of color every now and then."

"No, thanks." Casey shifted from her knees to a squat, as she repacked her stuff. "I don't like how it feels on my face."

"Suit yourself." Amelia glanced over toward where Jake was still scolding his daughter and a let out a dreamy sigh. "I think I'm in love."

"What?" Casey fell back, her bottom hitting the ground with a dull thud. She followed her sister's gaze to Jake and Veronica. He looked so different from the first day when he'd come to the tour company asking for her. Then, he'd been so polished, so professional in his navy suit and styled hair. Now, in his khaki pants, boots, thick waterproof jacket and tousled hair, he was so much more masculine and appealing. And when he pulled his daughter into a hug, Casey's heart melted. Thankfully, he didn't withhold his love, even when angry. An admirable quality.

"I know. Crazy, huh?" Amelia said. "I mean, what would I do in Treasure Creek?

But still, there's something very appealing about him."

Casey jerked her gaze away from Jake and focused back on her sister. Her twin, yet so unlike her. A sharp stab of jealousy pierced Casey's heart, rendering her speechless. She fought to breathe, to think.

Amelia held up her hand. "And I do remember what you said about him raising his daughter. He shouldn't have to do it alone. The girl clearly needs a woman to guide her through life. And Jake needs a wife."

So Amelia really was setting her sights on Jake. Along with the jealousy, a disturbing dose of disappointment and glumness invaded Casey. Whatever mixed signals Jake had been sending to Casey, apparently Amelia had deciphered and was ready to act on. Just proving Seth's parting words the last night she'd seen him, "You'll never be half the woman your sister is."

Stifling that unwanted reminder, Casey asked, "You really care about Veronica?"

Why had the maternal gene skipped Casey?

Amelia shrugged. "She's okay. She adores me, so it's easy to be around her."

Casey frowned. "You mean, like a new toy? What happens when the adoration fades?"

"I'm sure Jake and I would figure it out. Maybe she'll like boarding school."

"Amelia!"

"Joking. Besides, what's it to you?"

"Right. It's none of my business." Hardening her resolve not to care, Casey heaved herself to her feet and grabbed her pack. Needing to get moving so she could focus on putting one foot in front of the other, she said, "Time to go."

She didn't wait for Amelia's reply. She tramped to where everyone else had gathered. "Pack up. Our lunch break is over."

Aware of Marie's startled gaze at her abrupt tone, Casey tried for a more gentle pitch. "This next leg of our trip will require going up and over that hill." She pointed north, to the other side of the lake. "Then around another lake before hitting Lindermen City for the night."

Casey started walking as the others fell into step behind her.

"Hey, wait up."

Biting her lip, Casey halted and turned, as Jake, pulling Veronica behind him, hurried to catch up. When he reached her, he said, "Casey, Veronica has something to say."

The girl stood at her father's side, head bowed and eyes downcast. "I'm sorry I put so much makeup on you." She lifted her head, her blue eyes flashing with defensivness. "But I still think it was pretty."

Casey believed her. Veronica's reference to the popular television show made sense. For a girl who wants to grow up to work in the fashion industry, emulating what she sees done on TV makes sense. Feeling less upset, she said, "I accept your apology."

Veronica looked up at her dad. "Can I go?"

Jake sighed. "Yes."

They watched her skip back to Amelia's side.

"She really didn't mean to embarrass you," Jake commented.

"Forget it," Casey said, too self-conscious now to dare glancing his way, and began to walk away.

He stayed her forward progress, pressing a gentle hand to her arm. "Hey, look at me."

Feigning a smile, she faced him. "I'm fine."

Searching her face with his dark, intense gaze, he said, "Just so you know. You don't need makeup. You're beautiful as you are."

As the others caught up, Jake stepped back, resuming his spot at the rear of the group. Casey forced herself to break eye contact so she could lead the way. And if she'd had wings on her feet she'd have been soaring rather than hiking.

A few hours later, the trail dropped down the hillside between Long Lake and Deep Lake. Jake drank in the beauty of the stunning, vivid blue of the lakes. Rocky outcroppings and islands scraped with greenery dotted the water. Sunlight dappled through the cloud cover and glistened on the water. Up ahead, Casey waited at the foot of another expansion bridge built over a large stream of icy rapids. From there the trail would take them to the far side of the lake and up another mountain.

Veronica slowed as they neared the bridge. Her eyes grew huge. Jake saw the mounting panic on her sweet face. Without a word, Casey held out her hand to the girl. With a slight hesitation, Veronica grasped Casey's outstretched hand and turned to take Jake's.

Affection for Casey unfurled in Jake's chest. Even after his daughter's antics, Casey still cared enough to know Veronica needed her to cross the bridge.

When they were across, they found Marie sitting on a rock, holding her ankle.

"She twisted it coming across the bridge," Doug explained, starting to unlace Marie's boot.

Casey hurried to the older woman's side. "Whoa, whoa. Don't loosen the boot. Once it comes off it might not go back on."

"Of all the dumb things for me to do," Marie said, her lined face grimacing with pain. "I mean, I climb boulders, make it over root-studded trails and loose rock, but I can't step right on a flat slat."

"Don't be so hard on yourself," Casey said, as she helped to retie the woman's boot. "You're tired and the bridge rocks."

Jake liked the calm assurance and steadfast way Casey dealt with the situation.

"Doug, she'll need a good walking stick," Casey said.

Doug didn't hesitate. "I'm on it." He took off at a run.

For a man his age, he moved pretty good. Jake wanted to be as agile in twenty-plus years.

"Let's get that foot elevated." Casey helped Marie angle her heel atop a good-size rock, and made her comfortable. "We'll take an hour break and then keep moving."

"I'm going to explore a bit," Stan said, as he took off with his camera, leaving his pack behind.

Since it looked as if they would be taking another respite, Jake decided to give in to the fatigue gathering at the edges of his mind, and found a flat, sandy spot to lay down, with his head propped up on his pack.

"Dad, I'm going to pick some wildflowers," Veronica said, heading toward the tree line.

"No. You need to stay with the group."

She rolled her eyes. "Dad, I won't go far."

He glanced at the tree line, gauging the distance. His gut said keep her close. But he struggled with holding on too tight or giving her some room. "Don't go beyond the trees."

With a groan, she dropped her pack and stalked away.

Jake watched her for a moment. *Keep her safe, Lord.*

He turned his gaze toward the lake, taking in the beauty of the crystal-blue water and the mountains reflecting on the surface. His mind wandered to Casey. The startled, pleased look in her eyes when he'd told her she was beautiful made him feel ten feet tall and like he could do anything. He'd never experienced the pure joy of making someone else happy with something as simple as a compliment. Most women he'd known found happiness in things he could buy. But Casey wasn't like most women. And he was finding that refreshing.

"May I join you?"

Jake tensed as Amelia didn't wait for him to answer before stretching out next to him. So much for resting. He senses went on guard around Amelia Donner. She was what his fraternity brothers would call a man-eater. Just like Natalie...

He just hadn't realized what she was really like, until it was too late. He'd been so enamored with her, flattered by her attention and had felt needed by her. And when she told him she was pregnant with his child, he'd gladly done the honorable thing and married her. It wasn't until after the ceremony that she showed her true colors. She turned into Mrs. Hyde, demanding, clingy and spending money they didn't have. Though in *her* mind, he was from money, so why didn't they have more? As miserable as their marriage had become, he'd had every intention of keeping his vows for as long as he lived. But she had other plans. Plans that shredded his heart and his trust.

He shuddered. Man, he so did not want to go down that road again.

"Beautiful, isn't it?" Amelia said. "Almost makes me wish we could stay here forever."

"Almost?"

Her sultry laugh filled his ears as she turned to look at him. "Well, you couldn't very well run your family's business from out here, now could you?"

"Point taken."

"You know, your daughter could use some female influence."

Jake slid her a glance. "She has my mother."

"Of course." Amelia propped herself up on an elbow. "But don't you get lonely?"

Uncomfortable with the direction the conversation was taking, Jake sat up and pushed to his feet. "I am going to go find my daughter."

Grabbing both his and Veronica's packs, Jake headed for the tree line. The forest here was drier than the rain forest they'd recently come through. The foliage was less dense, with lodgepole pines, subalpine firs and willows shading the ground. The peat-scented air filled Jake's lungs while he considered the vastness of the forest. Where was Veronica? His gaze scanned the area. She wasn't at the tree line, she wasn't near the lake or with Casey and the Caruthers.

A noise to his left drew his attention. Stan trudging back from his explorations.

"Did you see my daughter?" Jake asked, a mixture of anger and anxiety tightening his gut.

Stan shook his head. "No. But I got some good pictures of a moose and some white-tailed deer. And the birds. Man, I've got some winners here."

Uninterested in his pictures, Jake started calling out Veronica's name. Hopefully, she'd hear him and start back from wherever she'd wandered off to. Man, was she in trouble.

"Jake? Something wrong?" Casey asked, as she joined him near the trunk of a willow where he'd set down the packs.

"Veronica's missing."

## Chapter Eight

Concern spread over Casey's expression. "Does she have her whistle with her?"

Dread formed a knot in Jake's chest, constricting his breathing. "Not sure." He checked her backpack and found it tucked in a side pocket. "No." He ran a hand through his hair. "Why didn't I think to make sure she had it?"

Casey put her hand on his shoulder, the gesture both comforting and humbling. "We'll find her. I'll get the others to help." She jogged away.

Unease twisted in his stomach with an acid burn. He shouldn't have let her go off by herself. She was only twelve and not used to the wilderness. He took a deep breath, trying to calm himself. He was overreacting. Twenty minutes wasn't really that long.

*Please, Lord, bring her back to me safely.*

It occurred to him he always felt more like praying when life became difficult or circumstances seemed out of his control. Was it that way for most people? Did they ignore God until they needed him?

Jake vowed to start including God in his daily life from then on.

Casey, Stan, Amelia and Doug jogged over, kicking up a cloud do dust as, one by one, they skidded to a stop.

"Does everyone have their whistles?" Urgency in Casey's voice made a tremor of fear race down Jake's spine.

"I have mine," Stan said, holding it up.

"Me, too." Amelia hung hers around her neck.

"Got it," Doug said.

"Make sure they work," Casey said, before lifting her whistle to her mouth and taking a sharp breath. The high-pitched whistle blast echoed off the lake. Jake blew into his as the others did, as well. The shrill noise reverberated through Jake's skull.

"Marie will stay with the packs while she elevates her foot, and in case Veronica shows up." Casey grabbed Jake and Veronica's packs and handed them to Doug. "Do you mind running these back? And make sure her whistle works."

"Will do," he said, and jogged away with them.

"Okay, when Doug gets back, we'll break into two groups. Stan, you and Doug will head to the right. The three of us will head left. Spread out, but stay within sight of each other. If you need assistance, give three quick blasts on the whistle. If you find Veronica, give two blasts." She glanced at her watch. In the distance, the blast of Marie's whistle punctuated the air. "In twenty minutes, I'll blow my whistle once. Everyone answer with one blast. If we haven't found her in twenty minutes, we head back here."

"Then what?" Jake asked, as panic battered at him, dredging up awful images that he refused to think about.

"There's a ranger's cabin about a mile away. We'll get more help," she said, her gaze direct. "You have to keep it together, okay?"

He nodded. He'd never been in a situation

like this. Helplessness overwhelmed and engulfed him in its smothering surge. He fought hard to keep the tide at bay. He had to be strong for his daughter.

They fanned out, keeping a good distance between each other, yet maintaining visibility, shouting Veronica's name, their voices bouncing off the trees and filling the forest. Startled birds took flight. The scurrying of small animals in the underbrush underscored the voices.

With every step, Jake's agitation rose. Where was she? Had she run way because he'd yelled at her earlier? Was she lying hurt somewhere and couldn't call out? Had someone taken her? Had an animal attacked her? The thoughts were relentless. Between yelling out her name, Jake prayed with a fervency he'd never experienced before.

Three loud whistle blasts shrilled through the woodlands. Somewhere to his right. He bolted in that direction. Casey and Amelia on his heels, their feet pounding on the forest floor.

The blasts came again.

"This way," Casey yelled, veering north.

The terrain began to rise, becoming rocky. Huge boulders appeared ahead.

Jake's heart jumped into his throat at the sight of his daughter wedged in the crevice of two boulders, a huge mountain lion pacing in front of her. The cat's paws were huge, his body lean and agile. The golden fur covering its body was matted in spots. The black mask of around his eyes and mouth gave the beast a feral quality.

"Veronica!" Jake shouted, and started to rush forward, only to be yanked back by Casey. She was amazingly strong for a woman of her stature.

"No," she barked.

"Psst," Doug waved to them from behind the trunk of a subalpine fir. His face was pale and his hands shook.

"Everyone stay back," Casey said, in a low, composed voice. "I need you all to unzip your jackets and open them wide. Make yourself as big as you can." She unzipped her coat, demonstrating. "We're going to move in unison, around to the left, and then come at him making as much noise as possible."

Following her lead, they moved in tandem, flanking the big, golden cat on the left while making all kinds of noises and flapping their jackets like wings. The startled cat turned to face them, his yellow eyes seeming to assess them. The lips of his mouth reared back to show sharp teeth that could rip through human flesh like a knife through butter. The cat's deep, guttural growl bounced off the boulders. Jake's heart slammed against his ribs as he mimicked the growl and let out shouted whoops, flapping his jacket madly.

The snarling beast backed up and then turned and fled, its graceful loping covering ground rapidly, until it disappeared out of sight.

Jake rushed to Veronica and pulled her to his chest. Relief and fear and love shuddered through him, squeezing his lungs and tightening his throat. Tears burned the back of his eyes.

"Thank You, God," he said on a breath, and sagged against the boulder with Veronica safely clinging to him. He kissed the top of her head, then looked up at the woman whose calm and competent knowledge had saved his daughter's life. Casey stood back, watching them with a tender expression on her lovely face. Next to her stood her so-different twin.

Amelia bumped Casey with her shoulder. "You were pretty amazing, sis. That was *Man Vs. Wild* in the flesh. Bear Grylls would be proud."

A blush heightened the color on Casey's creamy cheeks. "Thanks. I think."

Veronica pulled back, her dirty tear-streaked face and her lips trembling. "I'm sorry, Daddy. I forgot my whistle."

"Are you hurt?" Jake asked, searching for an injury.

She shook her head. "No."

"What happened?" Amelia asked.

"The mountain lion was on top of the boulder. I wanted to get a better look, so I tried to climb up. But then he saw me and jumped at me, knocking me off the rock. I squeezed in there." She gestured to the crevice. "He pawed at me but he didn't reach me."

Jake hugged her tighter. "I'm just glad you're alive."

Gratitude and something more that he couldn't even name filled him as he met Casey's gaze. She'd known what to do, had stayed calm and in control. She was beyond amazing. He mouthed a *"thank you."*

The kindhearted, soft smile she gave him in return slid into his battered heart. And that was good and bad all rolled into one confusing, disturbing package.

## Chapter Nine

Morning came with welcome relief, after another tense night spent on high alert, not only because of the would-be thief but also because the mountain lion could easily decide to make them prey. Casey and Jake had stayed up, keeping the fire going. Doug had crawled out of his tent not long after midnight and Stan had joined them a while later.

As soon as the others awoke, they hastily had breakfast, broke camp and headed for the trail. Now they were making the push toward Bennett Lake, the final destination of their hike. Over the distance tree tops rose the tall steeple of St. Andrew's Church, the last remnant of the booming town that once had existed on the shores of Lake Bennett, pointing the way and announcing that civilization was just miles ahead.

"Where are we? In the desert?" Amelia asked, as the terrain turned dry and sandy.

"Actually, yes. Welcome to the world's smallest desert. Two hundred and sixty hectares, roughly one square mile of dry sand," Casey said, with a sweeping hand. People were always surprised by this section of land. Very few knew of its existence. "This is the aftermath of a glacier flow from the last ice age. The dry climate and the strong winds coming off Lake Bennett have created the dunes and prevented much in the way of vegetation to grow." She pointed to the tree line, where the many spruce trees showed signs of erosion, their bark roughened by the years of sand blowing across them. "You can see the sand encroaching into the forest, damaging the trees."

"This is spectacular," Stan said, over the click of the camera, capturing the beauty of the area.

Casey maneuvered to help Doug with Marie, as the older woman tried to navigate the soft sand with her bum ankle. "We can stay the night here and then take the train in the morning, or we can press on to the train station and hope we can catch the last run of the day," she said to the group.

There was no debate. Everyone agreed to press on through. Clearly, everyone including Casey wanted to get home. The stress from the thief and the mountain-lion sighting was taking its toll.

The miles went by and the sand receded, while the forest around the lake grew thicker amid the colorful purple-and-red flowers of the fireweed plants.

"What is that?" Veronica pointed toward the lone wooden-steepled structure rising above the trees.

"St. Andrew's Church." Casey led the group toward the historic old building. "This is the last of the Klondike gold-rush buildings in the area. Bennett was a booming town at one time."

"There's something very touching about it," Marie said, as Doug helped her hobble closer to inspect the abandoned church. Its once-beautiful stained glass windows were now boarded up.

"I've always thought so," Casey agreed.

"Hey, there's railroad tracks." Veronica's

excited voice carried on the air from Casey's right. "Where's the station?"

"We have to walk down the train tracks a few miles," Casey explained. "Let's take a few minutes, and then we'll need to keep going if we want to make the last train."

As the others took advantage of the respite, Casey walked past the church to a vantage point where the crystal-blue glacier waters reflected the mountains on the sun-dabbled surface. The sight never failed to inspire a sense of awe. She remembered the first time she stood in this spot, with Uncle Patrick at her side. He hadn't said a word, only put his hand on her shoulder as if he, too, felt the sense of wonder filling her soul.

Awareness prickled the fine hairs at the back of her neck. She didn't need to turn around to know Jake had come up behind her. She'd been acutely aware of him for days. "It's beautiful, isn't it?"

"Yes. A beautiful sight," Jake replied, from just past her right shoulder. He touched her hand, laced his fingers through hers and pulled her around to face him. "I didn't have a chance last night to properly thank you for saving Veronica."

Vividly aware of his electric touch sending sparks up her arm, she stared into his dark, unfathomable eyes. "You did thank me."

He lifted her hand to his lips and placed the gentlest of kisses on her knuckle. "I hope you realize how special you are."

Her breath hitched. How did she respond to that? No one had ever said anything so sweet to her before. A warm glow flowed through her.

"This adventure will never be forgotten. Neither will you," he continued. "I can't tell you how grateful I am for all you've done for Veronica and me." He took her hand. "You've been a godsend. I hope this isn't goodbye."

Casey blinked as his words sank in. Panic swamped her. It sounded like he wanted more than just a professional relationship. She couldn't deal with that right now. She put on her tour guide persona. "That's good to know. And if Alaska's Treasures can ever be of service to you and Veronica again, don't hesitate to contact the office."

He looked perplexed. Remorse pricked at her conscience. She broke eye contact on the pretext of glancing at her watch. "That train won't wait." She headed back toward the others without a backward glance, even though her heart was still looking back.

The station was teeming with activity when they arrived at the platform. Jake recognized some of the hikers as those who had passed them a few days ago. Casey wouldn't meet his gaze as she made arrangements for their passage back to Treasure Creek. And when the black diesel train arrived, she made sure everyone boarded and had seats before moving out of the club car and joining two other Alaska's Treasures tour guides.

Jake barely noticed the panoramic views as the train wound its way down the mountain pass. The ice-tipped glaciers, the vistas and deep gulleys held little appeal, as Jake went over and over the exchange with Casey by the church. He'd been trying to tell her how he felt about her and this trip. He wanted her to know how much he'd appreciated her attention to his daughter, her quiet confidence and gentle leading. He'd wanted to tell her how much he'd come to care for her. But she'd made it clear the feeling wasn't mutual. Very clear.

And why that hurt he didn't know.

\* \* \*

They arrived in Treasure Creek near midnight. The cold night seeped through Casey's jacket after the warmth of the train. Tired and desperately wanting to get home, shower and fall asleep in her own bed, Casey first had work to do to close out her tour.

"You go on," she told Amelia. "I have a few things to do first."

Amelia didn't need any further encouragement. She was in her rental and driving away before everyone else had even disembarked from the train. Casey was surprised Amelia hadn't waited for Jake. Maybe his appeal had worn off?

"You should make sure to see a doctor about your ankle tomorrow," Casey advised Marie, after helping the couple to their sedan.

"I already called from the train and have an appointment in the morning," Doug said, sliding behind the wheel. "Thank you for everything."

She waved goodbye.

From behind her, the unmistakable click of Stan's camera drew her attention. "Don't you ever stopping taking pictures?"

Stan laughed. "Nope." He held out his hand.

"Thanks for a grand time. I'll be sending Amy copies and will let her know if and when the pictures will run in a magazine."

Shaking his hand, Casey narrowed her gaze. "Just make sure there are no pictures of me, okay?"

He grinned. "Can't make that promise," he said, and loped away toward the Treasure Creek Hotel, a half a block down, on Treasure Creek Lane.

She turned to head toward the offices, spying Jake and Veronica getting into his black SUV. He paused, his hand on the back hatch. She fought the urge to go over to him. And if she did, she had no idea what she'd say. There didn't seem to be any more to be said. They would both go back to their separate lives. She raised a hand in farewell. After a heartbeat, he raised his chin to her, closed the hatch, and walked to the driver's side. He hesitated before climbing in. His gaze sought hers over the expanse of the parking lot. She felt the impact of those dark, quizzical eyes all the way to her toes.

Then he was sliding inside the car and driving way. Leaving Casey with an inexplicable, maddening sense of loss.

\* \* \*

"Here you go," Casey said, as she walked into Amy's office the next morning. She laid the rolled treasure map on the desk. "Sorry I wasn't able to find the treasure for you."

Amy stuck the map into her brown leather bag. "I appreciate that you tried. I'm just sorry you had a scare. Reed contacted Simon, but he never saw anyone matching your description come by. Reed thinks the guy must have come back down the mountain."

"I'm sure if he's here in town, Reed will find him."

"Too true. Reed is like a pit bull with a bone. Tenacious doesn't cover it," Amy said, with a rueful shake of her head.

"Care to share?"

A blush heightened Amy's cheek color. "Nothing to share."

Casey hid a smile. "If you say so."

"I do."

"We also came face-to-face with a mountain lion," Casey said, and gave her boss the rundown on the incident.

Amy's eyebrows shot up. "Oh, my. We'll need to let everyone know to keep a look out. Thank God Veronica's okay."

"It was nerve-racking, that's for sure."

Amy flipped open a day planner. "Would you be willing to babysit the boys next Saturday for a few hours while I get my hair done?"

"Of course. I'll take them to the barn."

The tour company had a stable of horses used for pack tours. One of Casey's favorite things to do was take one of the horses out by herself and just ride.

"You know they'd love that."

She did. And she loved them. Amy's boys were the closest she'd ever come to children of her own. An image of Jake flashed in her mind, and with it a deep longing, but she pushed both away. No, her sister had set her sights on him, and Casey had no intention of coming in in second place again, not even for the chance of motherhood. No matter how much her heart yearned for Jake.

Jake sat in the center pew with Veronica, as the Treasure Creek Christian Church choir started the first hymn of the morning services. He needed some peace this morning. He'd had two restless nights full of dreams—dreams where Veronica was torn apart by the mountain lion. Then it was Casey being clawed and ripped at. He'd awaken with terror still pumping in his veins.

Each time, he reached for his Bible and read until he grew drowsy. Then the process would repeat. He hoped to catch a moment of Pastor Michaels's time after services today, maybe during the church social hour. Hopefully, the pastor would have some remedy for Jake's nightmares.

Beside him, he listened to Veronica sing, her voice clear and strong. She looked so pretty and innocent, in a bright pink dress that had a collar and wide belt. Even with mismatching socks and her black-and-white Skechers, she looked older than twelve. He praised God that, even as sullen as she could get, she hadn't turned away from worshiping—though he knew he shouldn't take it for granted. One day she might rebel against their faith, too. But for now, he'd appreciate her willingness to attend church.

From the corner of his eye, he saw Veronica gesturing frantically. He shifted his gaze fully to see what had her attention and was surprised to see Amelia and Casey Donner sliding into the pew next to Veronica. He gave

Amelia a polite smile to her more enthusiastic one. Casey didn't meet his gaze but kept her eyes straight ahead.

She looked great. All fresh, clean and down-to-earth. Her dark hair was loose today, with soft natural waves. She wore a plaid button-down shirt, in a mix of greens and blues that brought out the crystal-blue color of her eyes.

As if sensing his regard, she shifted her gaze ever so slightly toward him, with a quizzical arch to her eyebrows.

He leaned forward, moving more fully into her line of vision, and smiled. Gratified to see a blush work its way into her cheeks, and the return of the smile she seemed unable to keep from showing, Jake returned his attention to the front.

An hour later the service finished, and the congregation filed out into the August summer sunlight bathing the lawn behind the church, where everyone gathered for the after-service social hour. A table had been set up with refreshments, and a small stage and podium sat near the church's back door. The congenial sounds of conversation and laughter filled the air.

Jake looked around, his gaze searching through the crowd for Casey. Ah, there she was. She stood off to the side, talking with several men. The familiarity and easy way she conversed made it clear she knew these guys well. And why shouldn't she be surrounded by men? She was an attractive, unmarried woman living in a town full of eligible bachelors.

The heat of jealousy flashed white-hot, searing his mind as his gut clenched. *Whoa. Where had that come from?* His sports coat suddenly was too hot and constricting.

He had no claim on her. Had no intention of laying claim, either.

So why did it bother him so much when Casey allowed one of the guys to lead her to the refreshment table?

## Chapter Ten

**W**as Casey dating him? They looked awfully chummy. Jake tugged at the collar of his button-down shirt.

Noticing his daughter at the table as well, Jake moved, telling himself he was only heading in the direction of the refreshments to collect his daughter. He plastered a smile on his face as he approached the table.

"Daddy, they have lemon bars," Veronica squealed, and popped a yellow square into her mouth.

"That's nice, honey," Jake replied, as his gaze landed on Casey. She had a small, empty plate in her hands as she contemplated the various offerings. "Morning, Casey."

She slid a glance his direction. "Nice to see you, Jake."

Pleased at the sincerity in her tone, Jake smiled.

"Here." The guy she was with plopped an oatmeal cookie on Casey's plate, taking her attention away from Jake. "My mom said to tell you stop by when you get a chance. She's got some decorations or something for you."

Jake narrowed his gaze with surprise at the tall, young man hovering near Casey. Feeling foolish for having mistaken the youth for a full-grown man, and even more foolish for thinking there was something between the kid and Casey, Jake said, "Hi, I'm Jake Rodgers."

The kid shook Jake's hand. "Rick Halversham. My dad works for you."

"Oh. Cool. I just recently returned to town, so I haven't met many of the employees."

"Rick is home for the summer. He attends college in Seattle," Casey explained, with a note of approval in her tone.

"Good for you. A college education will take you far in life."

Or back to your roots. Jake wondered why

Casey hadn't gone off to university after high school.

"Thanks. Hey, Casey, I better go. Nice meeting you, Mr. Rodgers," Rick said, and strode away.

"Nice kid," Jake commented.

"Yep. He want to me to train him to lead tours next summer, when he comes home." Casey stepped past Jake to get a glass of lemonade.

He followed her, grateful she was talking to him. He hadn't been sure she would, after their last conversation. "Here, let me," he said, and reached for the cup.

She paused, eyed him for a moment and then allowed him to fill the cup. When he offered it to her, her fingers brushed his, sending a little zing through his system, all the way to his toes.

"I'd love some lemonade," Amelia said, from behind them.

Jake poured some into the cup he held and handed it to Amelia. "Here you go."

"Thank you, Jake. There are so few gentlemen left in the world." She sipped from the cup and gazed at him over the rim, with an appreciative gleam.

Ignoring her flirtation, Jake shifted his attention to his daughter. Her plate was piled high. "Veronica, that's enough sugar."

Veronica made a face. "It's just one of each."

"And the calories each one has will add inches to your hips," Amelia stated, with a derisive tone.

The incredulous look on Veronica's face made a knot form in Jake's chest. He really didn't need his daughter stressing about calories or inches.

He'd thought the sophisticated Amelia Donner would be a good influence on Veronica. But she was cut from a cloth that too closely resembled his ex-wife. He opened his mouth to blast Amelia for putting such negativity in his daughter's head, when Casey touched his arm, halting his words.

"Amelia!" Casey said, with censure in her tone.

Amelia raised her eyebrows in surprise. "What? What's wrong with the truth?"

How could these two very different women be twins?

Casey's beautiful eyes blazed as she glared at her sister. "She's twelve. She doesn't need to worry about calorie intake." Casey focused on Veronica. "However, that much sugar at one time isn't good for you, any way you look at it. I'm sure your dad will let you take your plate home for later."

Jake covered Casey's hand with his own, as gratitude filled him. "Of course. You can have a few cookies now, and save the rest."

Looking glum, Veronica said, "Fine."

"Excuse me, everyone." A female voice sounded over the PA system. A red-haired woman stood at the podium on the stage. She was cute, in a girl-next-door kind of way, with jeans and a flowered sweater. She was a bit older than Jake, more Reed's age.

Amelia slid her arm through his and gave her sister a pointed look. "Who's that?" she asked. Her voice held a sharp edge to it.

Just what was that about?

"Amy James, my boss," Casey replied, as she extracted her hand from beneath his. The loss of her warm touch made the mild summer air seem cooler to Jake.

Jake knew Amy a little, knew she was the woman whom Reed had proposed to. Jake wondered what the story was between them. And why the widow had said no.

"I know it's still summer, but we need to plan ahead. As most of you know, we always have a Christmas pageant, and I'm looking for volunteers to help. We have several areas where you all can get involved. This is a special program for our community, and it will take all of us to make it happen. We have four months to prepare, so it shouldn't be a burden for anyone. If you are interested, please come see me."

Claps and cheers followed Amy away from the podium.

"That sounds like fun," Amelia said, her gaze on Jake. "I could probably come home for Christmas, with the right incentive."

Jake blinked at the obvious suggestion in her tone. He swallowed back unease as his gaze desperately sought Casey for help.

She stared at him a moment, with a question in her eyes, before she focused on her sister. Tugging on her arm, Casey said, "Amelia, let's go say hello to Amy."

*Whew.* Jake let out a relieved breath as Casey drew Amelia away. The last thing he needed was the wrong twin gunning for him.

He grew still. *Wrong twin? As in Casey was the right one?*

When had that happened? And what was he going to do about it?

"Sign me up," Casey said to Amy, as she approached with her twin in tow.

Amy grinned. "I already have you down."

Casey laughed.

Turning her gaze to Amelia, Amy held out her hand. "It's good to see you again, Amelia. Casey talks about you often."

Giving Amy's hand a quick shake, Amelia said, "Don't believe a word she tells you."

Casey shot her sister a glare. "Amelia."

Amelia blinked at her. "Joking." To Amy, she said, "If I end up here at Christmastime, I'll help out, as well."

Amy's eyebrows rose. "Oh, lovely." She turned her quizzical gaze on Casey. "Won't that be lovely?"

Forcing herself not to make a face, Casey met Amy's gaze. "Lovely." Especially if Amelia coming home for Christmas meant Amelia and Jake were a couple. But the near-panicked look on his face when Amelia hinted at wanting him to be the reason for her return had Casey wondering. Maybe Jake wasn't as taken with Amelia as she had thought. Who knew?

"Where are the boys?"

Taking the hint to change the subject, Amy gestured toward the far side of the lawn, where several tables and chairs had been set up. "Over there, with Karenna and Gage."

"Ah." Casey spotted the munchkins, their happy little faces beaming. Karenna Digby, soon to be Mrs. Gage Parker, had a boy on each knee. The pretty blonde was flanked on one side by her cousin Maryann Jenner, a petite brunette with a bob haircut, fringy bangs and pale brown eyes. Karenna and Maryann had both been drawn to Treasure Creek by the *Now Woman* magazine article. And for Karenna, she'd found her perfect bachelor in hunky Gage Parker, one of Treasure Creek's search-and-rescue team members and a fellow Alaska's Treasures tour guide.

Pastor Michaels walked up. "Excuse me, ladies, I need to steal Amy for a moment."

"No problem," Casey said, and waved Amy away, as the pastor whisked off to speak to others who wanted to volunteer.

"Did you see where Jake went?" Amelia

asked, as she rose on tiptoes, her gaze searching the thinning throng of churchgoers. "Oh, I see him."

Casey watched her sister weave her way through the crowd to where Jake was talking with Reed Truscott. From the serious expressions on the men's faces, Casey didn't think Amelia interrupting them would be welcomed. She sighed and figured she'd better head Amelia off, then hurried after her.

Catching up to her twin just seconds before she inserted herself into Jake and Reed's conversation, Casey snagged Amelia's elbow and steered her toward Veronica, who had taken a seat on a bench.

Pulling her elbow away, Amelia groused, "What was that about?"

"Look, Veronica is by herself." Casey sat beside the girl. "When do your grandparents return from their cruise?"

"Dad's driving to Juneau this afternoon to pick them up," she said.

"Yoo-hoo, Casey? Casey Donner?"

Casey turned toward the high-pitched call. Her eyes widened as a woman looking sorely out of place came hurrying over. Her red ringlets bounced about her shoulders, emphasizing her short, curvy stature. With each step her spiky heels sank into the ground and she had to yank a bit to tug them free, making her look like she had some sort of walking impediment. Her formfitting, skinny-leg jeans and puffy down coat didn't help her any.

Amelia snickered. "Oh, dear. Where's the fashion police?"

Veronica giggled. "Good one."

Casey shot the two a quelling look as the stranger stopped in front of Casey.

"You're Casey Donner, aren't you?" The woman's bright pink lips spread into an expectant smile.

Not sure what to make of this woman, or the fact that she was seeking her out, Casey said, "I am. What can I do for you?"

"Well." She glanced at Amelia. "Oh, well. Now I understand."

Amelia arched an eyebrow. "Understand?"

The woman shifted her gaze back to Casey. "I was told you were a twin, and when I asked how I would know which of you to talk to, Harry said I'd know."

"Glad that was cleared up," Amelia muttered, and rolled her eyes. "Should I know Harry?"

"The proprietor at The General Store," Casey said, wondering just what Harry and this woman had talked about.

"Ah, him." Amelia wrinkled her nose. "He is a crab. Even when we were young he was a crab."

"Total crab," Veronica agreed.

"You had a question, Miss...?" Casey prompted.

"Delilah Carrington. I'm newly arrived in Treasure Creek."

Casey had a bad feeling in the pit of her stomach. "You came because of the article?"

"Why, yes! It was fascinating to read about you." Delilah lowered her voice, which really wasn't all that low, and ruined the conspiratorial effect she obviously was going for. "I was hoping you could give me some pointers."

Teeth setting on edge, Casey managed to say, "Pointers?"

"You know, how to hook one of these ruggedly handsome Alaskan men."

Amelia let out a bark of laughter. Casey couldn't stop her own mouth from twitching. "Uh, you do have the wrong twin." She pointed to Amelia. "She's the one who'd know about that."

Pulling herself together, Amelia puffed up. "I am an expert when it comes to men. Was there one in particular you were interested in?"

"Well, originally I was thinking of the local oil baron, but I understand he has a child. A teen, no less. I'm not looking to be an instant mother of a teenager."

Fully expecting her to have said Nate, or the handsome town pediatrician Alex Havens, Casey sucked in a shocked breath.

Veronica choked on a cookie.

Amelia stared hard at the woman, until Delilah backed up a step.

Casey rose as anger flushed through her. "This is Veronica, the oil baron's daughter. And anyone would be blessed to be her mother."

Clearly flustered, Delilah said, "Oh! Oh, my." Slanting an apologetic smile to Veronica, she said, "Sorry. Didn't mean to offend."

Veronica shrugged, her big blue eyes wide with curiosity. "No big deal."

Let off the hook, Delilah turned back to Casey. "I don't think the men in these parts are used to a woman like me. So I was thinking maybe you could tell me how to be like you."

Casey tucked in her chin, not sure how to take the request. "Like me?"

Delilah brightened. "You know." She made air quotes. "'One of the guys'." She shrugged. "I figure maybe if I changed, became less—" She made a sweeping gesture at herself. "Me, I'd have a chance. You see, my thirtieth birthday is right around the corner, and I have to be married before then."

"Why before then?" Amelia asked, an odd look flashing across her face.

"Please," Delilah intoned. "I have no intention of ending up a spinster. And no man wants a wife once they've turned the corner." She made a face. "Besides, I made a pact with—" she let out a long-suffering sigh "—a friend that I'd marry him if I wasn't already married by my birthday."

Insulted and amused at the same time, Casey shook her head. "Sorry. I can't help you."

"Really?"

By the incredulous look on Delilah's face,

Casey guessed the woman wasn't told "no" often. "Really."

Delilah's shoulders sagged. "I guess I'll have to find another way." She wandered away, obviously disappointed, if her rounded shoulders were any indication.

As soon as she was out of earshot, Veronica said, "That was so weird."

Casey pinched the bridge of her nose, exasperated by the attention from the article and the insensitive man hunters. "You have no idea."

Monday morning, Casey arrived at work to find the place buzzing. She stopped the receptionist, Rachel, in the hall. "What's going on? Why is everyone here?"

"Amy called an emergency meeting," Rachel said. "She wanted *everyone*, even the part-timers with other jobs, to come in. We're to gather in the break room."

Anxiety arced through Casey. The last time they'd had an emergency meeting that required pulling part-time tour guides from their other jobs had been when Ben passed away.

As Casey she hurried after Rachel, the need

to reach out to God overwhelmed her. *Please, God, no deaths.*

Casey slipped into a chair next to the local pediatrician and part-time rafting tour guide, Alex Havens. "Do you know what this is about?" she asked, figuring, as a doctor, he'd have information if the meeting was about anything dire.

Alex shook his head, his chestnut-brown hair falling across his forehead. His baby blues reflected the concern filling Casey. "I don't. I just came when I got the summons. Though, I hope this doesn't take long." He shifted his attention forward as Amy held up a hand, effectively quieting the room.

Her usually creamy complexion was pale, and dark circles marred the skin beneath her bright blue eyes. "Last night my great-grandfather's map disappeared from my house. I think someone stole it."

A collective gasp followed by exclamations of concern and outrage bounced off the picture-covered walls. Everyone in town was protective of Amy and the boys. Amy again held up her hand for silence.

"Were you or the boys hurt?" Gage Parker asked, his scowl fierce, letting everyone know he was ready to pound on someone if the kids had been injured. Big and brawny, the man was even an intimidating figure when he wasn't upset. He'd been one of Ben's close friends, and took watching out for his friend's widow and kids seriously.

Amy sent him a warm smile. "No. We're all fine. Just a bit shook up. I had the map out on the kitchen table next to a topography map, trying to make sense of the thing, when I went into the living room to answer the phone. When I returned to the kitchen, the map was gone and the back door was wide open." She gave her head a shake, sending her red curls bouncing. "Teach me to lock my doors."

Pushing back his Stetson, Nate asked, "So what now?"

"Chief Truscott is looking into the theft. I gave the one copy I had to Peter Stiles, who's taking a rafting tour group out this morning. So, if anyone can recreate the map, that would be great. I can't tell you all how much finding that treasure means to me. To the town. The influx of tourists, drawn to our town by the magazine article, can't last forever. I'm praying that the treasure will be the town's saving grace. We need that map back, so I need you all to be on alert. If you hear or see anyone with the map, please let the chief know."

Alex rose. "That's a shame. I'll keep watch for the map. But now I need to get out to the Taiya village." He addressed the room at large. "Just so you are all aware, there's a chicken pox outbreak. If you haven't had them, please be careful."

"That doesn't sound good. Is there anything I can do to help?" Casey asked. She enjoyed visiting the native village of the Tlingit tribe—especially in the month of November, during Alaska Native Heritage Month, when there were many different educational speakers, and a festival with traditional food and entertainment. The warm and friendly people were exceptional craftsmen. Casey had several intricately woven baskets she'd purchased over the years and used regularly.

Alex smiled, his handsome face lighting up. "I'm in need of a nurse. Can you give shots?"

Casey screwed up her nose. "No. I don't like needles."

He gave her a rueful grin. "Thanks for the offer anyway," he said.

Nate rose and clapped Alex on the back.

"Good of you to see to the children, Doc. We all appreciate you."

A red stain crept up Alex's neck. "Thanks," he said, gruffly, and headed out the door. Amy followed him, peppering him with questions on what to do if the boys came down with the disease.

"We'll miss him when he's gone," Andy Carlson said, from the back of the room.

Casey turned to the older gentlemen who was now retired from the post office, and who'd been a tour guide since the beginning of the company.

"What do you mean?"

"You know, the government paid to put Doc Havens through med school, and in repayment he had to practice here," Andy explained, his grey eyes sad. "But he only has a few more months left on his three-year contract."

"You don't think he'll stay?" asked Ethan Eckles, a thirty-something tour guide who also was a local grade school teacher during the school year.

"Naw. He's itching to get back to the lower forty-eight. Or at least, wherever he's from," Nate said, with a bit of derision in his tone, making it clear he wasn't a fan of the lower majority of the country.

"Los Angeles, I heard tell," Andy said, with a shake of his head. "City folk. They just don't get it."

Several heads nodded in agreement. For born-and-bred Alaskans, there was no place better on earth than where they were. God's country.

Rachel hovered close by, with pencil and paper. Casey held out her hand. "I'll try to sketch what I remember about the map the best I can. But I'm no artist."

Rachel grinned. "No worries. I am. I plan to take whatever anyone remembers and merge the descriptions into one."

"I didn't know that you were an artist, Rachel," Casey said, with a smile, as she settled with the paper and pencil. She closed her eyes, visualizing the map. A few minutes later, she had a crude drawing to hand back to Rachel.

"Nicely done," Rachel commented.

Casey wasn't so sure. "Where's Amy?"

"Chief Truscott just arrived, and they are in her office."

Deciding now wasn't a good time to check

on her friend, Casey headed to her cubicle. The message light on her phone blinked. She hit the button to listen to the message.

"Casey, it's me, Jake. Jake Rodgers."

Jake's voice sent shivers of surprise running over her arms. She swallowed hard. Her nerve endings buzzed.

"I was wondering if you were free next Saturday night. We missed the last church barbeque, and I thought maybe we could go to the next one. Together. To the barbeque."

The uncertainty in his voice made her smile. But his request was out of the question for her, considering how tied up in knots she was, just hearing his voice. Going on a date, even just to the singles group barbeque, wasn't a good idea. Better to nip this in the bud now, before she let her heart get attached.

She quickly dialed back the number he left. On the third ring, the call went to voice mail, so she left a message.

"Hi, Jake, it's Casey. Hey, thank you for the invitation. But I have to pass." She paused. Was that too abrupt? Should she try to explain? What could she say? *Sorry, I don't date, even though all I really want is to find a man like you and have a family, but there was too much to risk, too much hurt.*

Too much heartache down that path.

Lame. But the truth.

The shrill sound of the voice mail reaching the end of its time startled her.

Wincing, she hung up and hoped she'd hadn't just made the biggest mistake of her life.

## Chapter Eleven

Jake's cell phone beeped, indicating he had a voice mail. The call must have come in while he was getting ready for the office. Excusing himself from the kitchen table where he, his parents and Veronica were just finishing up breakfast, he stepped out onto the back porch to listen.

At the sound of Casey's voice, his pulse sped up.

But as he heard the message, heard her say no to his invitation to go to the church's barbeque, the air hissed out of his lungs like a gas leak. Putting the brakes on his reaction, he pushed the spiraling disappointment aside and decided her refusal was for the best.

Concentrating on getting his daughter

acclimated to life in Alaska had to be his priority. Complicating his life with a romance wasn't a good plan. Letting himself fall for Casey Donner wasn't smart.

Too bad his heart was feeling stupid.

After a frustrating week of only leading a few day hikes, Casey brought Amelia with her to the school gymnasium, where preparations for their class reunion were underway. Casey was glad to help out. But she really had no desire to attend the function, when she knew she'd probably end up taking more ribbing about the magazine article from her former classmates.

She was conflicted between wanting the fervor of the article to die down and wanting more people to read the magazine and come to Treasure Creek. Sacrificing her self-esteem for the town seemed a small price to pay. But deliberately putting herself in an uncomfortable situation was something she could control.

Her attention snapped to her sister and the head of the decorations committee as they squared off.

"I think we should do a black-and-white

theme," Amelia inserted, drawing everyone's gaze. "Something sophisticated and up-to-date."

"We've already decided on the theme. 'Following the Yellow-Brick Road Home,'" Renee Haversham shot back, her green eyes flashing. "It's too late to change now."

The four other women on the committee backed up Renee with nods of agreement.

Amelia made a face. "It's a bit juvenile, if you ask me."

"Nobody's asking," Renee said, her gaze challenging.

Casey could feel the animosity growing with every second, filling the school gymnasium with a cold front. She'd known bringing Amelia with her to the meeting would be awkward, but she hadn't anticipated how tense the situation would become.

From the moment Casey and Amelia walked in, the other women, usually so friendly and upbeat, had closed ranks, making it clear they didn't appreciate Amelia's input. Casey didn't blame them. Her sister wasn't exactly tactful in her derision of their efforts.

Feeling the need to alleviate the tension, Casey took Amelia by the arm. "Why don't you help me make the paper rosettes for the banner and let everyone else get back to what they were doing?"

Renee sent Casey a grateful smile before addressing the other women. "Table centerpieces? Gail, you said you had an idea."

Dragging Amelia away, Casey said, "Could you just try to get along for once?"

Amelia snorted. "I didn't get along with these girls in high school. What made you think I would now?"

Frustration pounded at Casey's temple. "But you said you wanted to come. You knew who would be here."

Amelia rolled her eyes. "Whatever. Let's make rosettes."

The door to the gymnasium opened and framed the outline of a man backed by the August sun. Then he stepped inside. Big, blond and classically handsome, like some movie star, but Casey didn't recognize him. She was sure he hadn't attend Treasure Creek High.

Amelia let out a small gasp before turning and fleeing out the side door. Casey stared after her sister. *Amelia turning tail and heading for the brush? Very odd.*

When Casey returned her attention to the blond man now talking with Renee, Casey had a feeling she now knew whose calls her sister had been dodging. The tall man in sophisticated, light-colored slacks, loafers and a button-down shirt beneath a sports jacket looked very out of place for Treasure Creek. And Renee pointing in her direction only confirmed this man's presence had something to do with Amelia.

Feeling protective, Casey pasted on a smile as the man approached. His light gray eyes searched her face before he held out his hand.

"I'm Gregory Stratton. I'm looking for Amelia," he said in a clipped British accent.

"I'm Casey, her sister. Why are you looking for Amelia?"

A sad smile curved his lips. "She didn't tell you?"

Something about the hangdog expression on his chiseled features pulled at Casey. "No. But that's not unusual. You are a friend?"

He let out a small laugh. "Yes. Nothing sinister going on here."

"Then what?"

"As much as I would like to rally your

help as an ally, I know Amelia well enough to know she'd be upset if I talked out of turn. Suffice it to say, I wish to speak with her on a personal matter."

"Personal matter," Casey repeated. Right. As in, this man was in love with Amelia, or what? "Where are you staying?"

"The Treasure Creek Hotel."

"Well, Gregory, I'll make sure to let my sister know."

"I would appreciate it," he said, with a curt tip of his head, before he left the way he'd come.

Aware of the curious stares, Casey gathered up the paper rosette supplies. "Renee, I'm going to take all of this home and work on it there."

And while she was at it, she'd make her sister spill her guts. Casey carried the box to her car, half expecting to see Amelia sitting inside, but she wasn't. Boy, her sister was really motivated to stay out of sight if she *walked home*. Not that it was that far. Casey and Amelia had walked to school most days, but considering that her sister had been wearing fancy shoes with heels, her walking home was a surprise.

When Casey pulled into the driveway of her home she found Veronica standing on the porch stairs. A white ten-speed bike leaned against the railing.

"Hi, what are you doing here?" Casey asked, as she carried her supplies up the stairs.

"I wanted to ask Amelia something," the girl said.

"Does your dad know you're here?"

"I let Grandma know." Veronica looked past Casey. "Amelia's not with you?"

"She was. But I guess she isn't home yet," Casey stated, setting her burden down so she could unlock the door. Where had Amelia gone? Concern bubbled. Surely her sister would return soon. Where else would she go? Maybe she'd decided to face Gregory Stratton after all. Curiosity burned in Casey's veins.

Veronica grabbed the box of rosette supplies and carried it inside. As Casey started to shut the front door, the distinct sound of drawers slamming shut stilled her hand. The noise was coming from Amelia's room. She was home after all.

"I'll be right back," Casey said to Veronica, and hurried down the hall.

When she entered Amelia's room, Amelia had her suitcases on the bed and was throwing her clothes in willy-nilly. So unlike her ultra-clothes-conscious twin, who hated wrinkles and usually wrapped each piece of clothing in plastic before packing it.

Casey rushed forward, grabbed Amelia by the shoulders and forced her to stop her frantic movements. "Amelia, what is going on?"

"I need to leave." Amelia tried to jerk away.

"No. You need to tell me what is going on. Who is Gregory Stratton?"

"I can't believe he came." Amelia's eyes grew wide. "He's not here, is he? I heard someone knocking."

"No, Veronica's here." Casey drew Amelia to the edge of the bed and gently pushed her to a sitting position. "Talk to me."

Amelia shook her head. "You wouldn't understand."

"Try me."

Taking gulping breaths, Amelia said, "Greg is my boyfriend."

So Casey had been right. Gregory's feelings for her sister had been obvious. But did Amelia feel the same? "*Boyfriend?* I'm confused. You haven't mentioned him at all. Ever." She narrowed her gaze on her sister's face. "What was all that flirting with Jake about during the past few weeks?"

With a dismissive wave, Amelia said, "Just flirting. No big deal."

Maybe not to her. Unbelievable. "Is Gregory why you came home three weeks early?"

"Yes. He asked me to marry him."

Shock siphoned the blood from Casey's head. Marriage? Amelia settling down? The thought sent her mind reeling. She pushed aside the suitcase on the bed to sit beside Amelia. "Okay. Let me get this straight. He asked you to marry him and you said…?"

Giving her a hangdog look, Amelia admitted, "I didn't give him an answer."

Who was this woman sitting here, and where had her strong-willed, decisive sister gone? "Apparently, he wants one. I take it he's the one that's been calling your cell phone."

Amelia nodded. "He won't give up until I give him an answer."

"Well, an answer would be good." Casey wasn't sure what to make of this development. This was such a different side to Amelia. "Do you love him?"

Amelia bit her lip and tears welled in her eyes. "I think so." She gripped Casey's hand. "But Casey...I don't know how to have a lasting relationship. I'm afraid."

Casey's heart contracted. "I understand. Oh, Amelia." She wrapped her arms around her twin and hugged her tight. "I do understand, but I never would have guessed you were as tortured by the same fear as me."

Amelia pulled back and narrowed gaze on Casey's face. "Is that why you don't have any serious boyfriends? Because you're *afraid?* Is that why you and Seth didn't work out?"

Casey's stomach roiled. She let go of her sister and eased away. "Yes and no."

"Explain."

"He wanted more than I was willing to give without being married."

Realization dawned in Amelia's expression. "Right. You've always been the perfect girl."

"I'm not perfect!" Casey said. "Are you *kidding?* I have my faults. But that was one thing I couldn't compromise on—no matter how much the world says having sex before marriage is normal and expected. No matter what holding on to my beliefs cost me."

The price had been her ability to trust in love.

Seth had started out so caring and considerate; but as the weeks progressed, he'd become more demanding of her time and energy. Constantly pushing her boundaries until one night, he'd given her an ultimatum—she either put out or lost him.

His love had been conditional. Saying no had been the hardest test of her will she'd ever endured. A test she had vowed never to repeat.

Amelia squeezed her hand. "I'm proud of you for holding out for marriage." Her gaze dropped to their joined hands. "Sometimes I wish I could go back and redo my life."

The regret in her sister's voice broke Casey's heart. She wished she could grant her that wish. But she couldn't. The past couldn't be unwritten. They only had control over the future.

"Amelia, Gregory deserves the truth. You need to tell him how you feel. And then go on from there."

Amelia blew out a breath. "I know you're right."

"He's staying at the Treasure Creek Hotel."

"Thanks," Amelia, said and rose. "We're quite a pair, aren't we? Both afraid to commit."

"But at least you try," Casey said, ruefully.

Amelia grinned. "True."

Casey grabbed a pillow and threw it at Amelia.

Sobering, Amelia said, "Seth wasn't good enough for you anyway. The guy was a jerk."

"He told me, you and he had…" Casey bit her lip, hating to reveal how hurt she'd been by his revelation.

Amelia wrinkled her nose. "What? No. I have my standards. Even back then."

For some reason, the knowledge her sister hadn't had an intimate relationship with Seth lifted the resentment Casey hadn't consciously acknowledged she'd been carrying all these years. Casey didn't even take offense at the implied insult. It didn't matter. It was in the past.

Casey stood and moved toward the door

but paused to look at Amelia. "What about Jake?"

Amelia's gaze sharpened. "He's dreamy. Now, that's the kind of guy you'd do well to marry."

Casey choked on a surprised and embarrassed laugh. "Me? You've been dogging his trail the whole time you've been here."

"Yes, I have. I'm sorry. It was a lame attempt to forget Gregory." Amelia sighed. "No luck. Besides, like Delilah said, I'm not cut out to be a ready-made mom of a teenager."

"But Veronica dotes on your every word."

"True. I'm just not ready to be a mom." A gleam entered Amelia's eyes. "But an aunt? Now there's a role I could get into. I realized early on that Jake likes you. You just need to give him a chance."

Knowing Amelia's words were easier said than done, Casey tucked her arm through Amelia's and led her from the room. "Come on, you've got people to see."

"Chicken," Amelia said on a laugh.

As they entered the living room, Veronica bounded out of the kitchen chair. "Amelia, hi."

"Hey, kid." Walking past Veronica, Amelia

picked up her purse and dug around inside. "Casey, have you seen my keys?"

"In the basket by the front door. I found them last night on the kitchen counter." Casey blocked Amelia's way. "Veronica came to see you."

"Right." Amelia turned to the young girl. "Did you need something?"

"I was hoping you'd help me with some fashion advice. I've been invited to a 'before the school year starts party,'" Veronica said.

"Oh. Can't help you now. Maybe later." Amelia grabbed the keys to her rental from the intricately woven basket and walked out the door without another word.

Casey blinked, then clenched her teeth. Frustration welled inside her. Amelia was Amelia. Casey couldn't expect her to change in one fell swoop. Putting on a smile, Casey turned to Veronica. "I'll help if I can."

Veronica's shoulders slumped. "That's okay."

Hoping to take the sting out of her sister's rude exit, Casey said, "Since you're here, I could use some help."

In a glum voice, Veronica said, "What?"

Moving to the box she'd brought in, Casey

pulled out a yellow paper flower. "I have to make rosettes—*hundreds* of rosettes—for my high school reunion decorations. Would you have time to help me out?"

"Sure. I've got nothing else to do."

Stifling a smile at the self-pity in the girl's tone, Casey explained the process and soon they were busy making the yellow flowers. As they worked, Casey initiated the conversation, and soon Veronica was chatting away about her old school, the kids there, her worries about being a new kid at school, which started on just two weeks, and about her dad.

On the subject of Jake, Casey couldn't stop her curiosity about the man, and she had to force herself not to ask revealing questions.

A knock at the front door startled them both. Casey put aside the flower she was in the middle of making to answer the door. She blinked in surprise and her heart did a little cartwheel to see Jake on her porch. His tie was slightly askew, his expression reflecting a mixture of worry and wariness as his dark eyes searched her face.

Concern replaced her surprise. "Hi. Are you okay?"

He gave a terse nod. "Is Veronica here?"

Opening the door wider, Casey stepped back. "She is. Come in."

Jake stalked forward, like a man about to go to battle, only, dressed in his business suit, his battlefield would be the boardroom. "Veronica, you had your grandmother worried out of her mind."

Casey stared at the girl and watched red bloom in her cheeks. "I thought you said you'd told your grandmother where you were going?"

Hanging her head in sheepishness, Veronica said, "I left her a note."

"Which she didn't find until about fifteen minutes ago," Jake stated, his voice hard and irritated. "You can't just take off like that, Veronica. You don't know the area well enough to be out on your own. Didn't the mountain lion teach you anything?"

"I was bored."

"So instead you'd rather put your grandmother through the torture of not knowing where you went?"

Veronica lifted her head, her eyes filled with tears. "Grandma was resting. I didn't want to disturb her."

"You could have at least left the note where

she'd find it, not sitting on the counter under a piece of fruit."

Casey could see Jake was holding on to his patience by a thread. She wasn't sure she should interfere in this family issue, but they were in her house, and if she didn't defuse the situation soon, Veronica's visit would turn into a much bigger deal. "What would have been a better choice, Veronica?" Casey asked.

Veronica shifted her gaze to meet Casey's. She was quiet for a moment as she thought. "Call Dad?"

Jake planted his hand on his hips. "That would have been helpful."

"I didn't think about it," Veronica replied, her voice rising slightly. "Please, Daddy, I'm sorry."

The fire seemed to drain out of Jake. He opened his arms to his daughter. She flew out her of chair and into his embrace. "I forgive you. Just don't let it happen again."

"I won't," came her muffled reply, against his chest.

Casey met Jake's gaze over Veronica's head and held it. A little thrill raced down her spine at the tender affection she saw there. "You should let your mother know Veronica's all right."

"Right." He released his daughter and pulled his cell phone out of his pocket and made the call. When he was done, he said, "We should probably go. I'm sure we've worn out our welcome."

Veronica hurried back to the table where the yellow rosettes were spilling out of the box. "But we're not done. Look. We're making flowers for Casey's high school reunion."

"She's been a big help," Casey said, wanting to help the kid earn some points with her dad.

"Maybe you can come back another time to help. Come on, honey. We should get home."

Veronica sighed and stood with a rosette in her hand. "I'm hungry."

Casey's heart clutched. She didn't want them to leave. She heard Amelia's voice in her head. *Chicken.* Then Amy's voice piped in. *Time for you to stop isolating yourself. Be open to a relationship.*

Dare she?

Before she let her doubts and fears talk her out of taking a chance, Casey said, in a rush,

"Would you two like to stay for dinner? I'm not sure when Amelia will be home. I'll be eating alone." She cringed at how lame and pathetic she sounded. Her breath trapped in her chest, she waited for Jake's response.

He cocked his head to the side. "Are you sure?"

No doubt he was thinking about how she'd turned him down when he'd asked her to the barbeque. Why would she want him to stay now? But that was before she'd seen her own fears of commitment and loss in her twin's eyes. Before she'd seen how miserable and irrational running away from a chance at love could make someone. She didn't want to run away anymore by isolating herself.

Today, here and now, she wanted Jake to stay so bad she could taste it. "I'm sure."

His expression softened, until a pleased smile teased his lips. "I—we'd…" He gestured to Veronica. "We'd love to." He opened his phone again. "I just need to let my parents know we won't be home for dinner."

"Great." Elated, Casey moved toward the kitchen with a light step. "Veronica, why don't you help me decide what we should cook?"

Within a few minutes they'd decided on

pasta with pesto sauce, salad and garlic bread. Casey was grateful her sister had stocked the kitchen. Normally, Casey wouldn't have had so much to choose from.

Setting water to boil, Casey directed Veronica on how to make the bread with real crushed garlic.

Jake entered the kitchen. He'd removed his tie and suit jacket. Rolling up his sleeves, he asked, "What can I do to help?"

"You could make the salad," Casey replied, liking that he wanted to help, and even more, how natural having these two people in her kitchen felt.

They worked around each other, busily cooking, and chatted, the subjects varying from books and movies to reminiscing about their hike. The conversation never let up all through the meal and fulfillment expanded in Casey's heart.

This is what she longed for. A family to call her own. She ignored the nagging voice trying to tell her to be careful, not to grow too attached. Jake and his daughter were not her family.

After dinner they moved into the living room, where Casey, unwilling to see them leave, dragged out some board games from the hall closet.

"I have Sorry!, Monopoly, Risk," she said, her arms laden with the games.

"Sorry!" Veronica said, with a huge grin.

"Sorry! it is." She set the games down and handed the requested game to Veronica to set up.

"Mind if I start a fire?" Jake asked.

"A fire would be great," Casey said. Memories of snuggling close to him for warmth in front of the campfire sent a warm glow through her.

As they began to play the board game, Casey sat back with a contented sigh. She could get used to this. But a nasty little voice inside her head whispered, *Are you really willing to take the risk?*

# Chapter Twelve

The evening couldn't have turned out more perfect if Jake had planned it. From the moment Casey had opened her door, he'd experienced this sense of calmness stealing through him. Something about Casey grounded Jake.

He'd been caught off guard when Casey invited them to dinner. He couldn't help but wonder why she'd changed her mind about spending time with him. He decided not to question her motives, and instead to be thankful.

Dinner and board games from back in the day were fine by him. He couldn't remember the last time he been so at ease. Raising a soon-to-be teenager and taking over the family business from his father was stressful enough. Adding worry over his friend Tucker to the mix had Jake wound up tight. This evening had been the perfect antidote.

And yet, the joy was bittersweet.

Nights like this were what he'd dreamed of having when he'd married and started a family. He'd done the best he could with Veronica, but most games were better played with more than two people.

"Decaf coffee?" Casey asked, pulling him from his thoughts.

"Love some." He stood. "Let me help."

Veronica curled up on the couch. "None for me, thanks."

Suppressing a smile, Jake replied, "Good to know." Like he'd let her have some anyway. Didn't coffee stunt growth? Or was that an old wives' tale?

When he joined Casey in the kitchen, she asked, "Sugar? Cream?"

"Black's fine." He leaned against the counter. "This has been great, Casey."

Her gaze was a soft caress. "It has been. Thank you for staying."

"Thank *you* for asking." He reached out to

brush back a stray hair that had fallen from her ponytail. "Why did you?"

A blush heightened the color of her cheeks. "I told you. I didn't want to be alone."

True, she'd said that, but he hoped that wasn't the only reason. "I don't think so."

She arched an eyebrow. "What *do* you think?"

"That you like me, but you're afraid to fess up." He crossed his arms over his chest to hide the fact that he was holding his breath and praying he was right.

She blinked, clearly disconcerted by his answer. "Of course I *like* you. You're a like-able guy," she stated, in a light tone that sounded a bit forced, then busied herself with the coffeemaker.

"My late ex would have disagreed," he muttered. "To her, I was a disagreeable, cold man who thinks only of himself." Her words had cut to the bone, true or not. And he had enough doubts to still bleed.

"Doesn't sound like she really knew you. I've seen a man who dotes on his daughter and who cares deeply for his friends," Casey said, her expression sincere.

Her words swept over him like a soothing balm. "We were so young when we married."

Her eyebrows drew together. "Why didn't you wait until after college to marry?"

A niggling of shame and guilt bit at him. "Natalie was pregnant."

The color drained from Casey's face. "Oh." She blinked several times, seeming to digest his words. "I see." She turned away to pour coffee in two mugs.

He hated that he'd been so careless, yet how could he say Veronica was a mistake? If he'd upheld the morals he'd been taught since childhood, Veronica wouldn't exist. Acknowledging that God used everything, even sin, to His purpose helped Jake come to terms with his past.

Handing him a mug, Casey asked, "You divorced before she passed away, isn't that right?"

"Yes." Uncomfortable suddenly with talking with Casey about wanting to stay married to a woman like Natalie, Jake hesitated. Being with Casey felt so right. His attraction to her was strong. Physically, no doubt—but even more on a heart level that he'd never felt before for anyone else. And that scared him a little.

Knowing that being open was the best way to proceed, he continued, "The divorce wasn't my idea. Natalie decided she didn't want to be a mother, nor the wife of a struggling college student. She left when Veronica was an infant. Luckily, the university had a child-care program."

Sadness crept into Casey's blue eyes. "That must have been so hard."

"It was. *Is,*" he corrected. "I moved us here because Veronica was reaching an age where she needs more family around. My parents are all we have."

"It's good you have them."

The wistful tone in her voice made his heart lurch. "You have your sister."

Her mouth tipped up on one corner in a feeble attempt at a smile. "Right. Since she's been home, we've grown a bit closer."

"That's something to thank God for."

When she didn't say anything, he let his burning curiosity loose and asked, "If you're so angry at God, why do you attend church?" She'd been in attendance at the Sunday morning service for the past few weeks. A fact he saw as a good sign. But he wanted it confirmed.

She moved past him to sit at the dining table, where she put her coffee mug aside to pick up a yellow paper rosette. "Because I thought about what you said. I figured it was time to start making my peace with God." When she met his gaze, tears had formed in her eyes.

Jake moved to squat down beside her. "He loves you, Casey."

*And so do I.*

The thought slammed into his consciousness. Tremors of shock rattled through Jake, nearly toppling him onto his backside. *Wow. Where did that come from? No idea.*

Okay, time to make an exit before he did something dumb, like say the words out loud.

Confusion swirled in Casey's brain. One moment Jake was next to her, his dear, handsome face so earnest as he declared God loved her, and then, next, he'd paled and abruptly stood, saying it was late, they needed to leave.

She followed him into the living room

where Veronica had fallen asleep on the couch. Jake stood there staring down at his daughter, his expression so gentle and full of love. An ache gripped Casey from deep within her being. She longed to be loved like that. Unconditional, unending.

*God loves you, Casey.*

Maybe she *was* loved like that.

A peacefulness calmed her, soothed the ache, but didn't make the need disappear completely.

She wanted a love, here on earth, with a man. A man like Jake.

Her heart jerked and fear reared its ugly head. Her mind grabbed on to the revelation he'd dealt her. Natalie had been pregnant before they'd married. Had Jake given her an ultimatum?

She hated to think he could be anything like Seth. But the fact remained, he'd married Natalie because she was already pregnant with his child.

Doubts assaulted her. Maybe she was the freak for believing that intimacy came after marriage.

She remained motionless as Jake scooped Veronica up into his arms and carried her toward the door. At the last second, her brain kicked in, and her limbs moved. She rushed ahead of Jake to open the door.

He paused, his eyes unreadable, as he said, "Good night, Casey."

"Good night, Jake." She shut the door behind him.

Sharp loneliness surged over her like the rapid, crushing flow of an avalanche down a mountainside. She felt weighted down, smothered, barely able to take a breath.

Pressing her back to the door, she closed her eyes. Words came slowly at first, but soon gathered momentum. All the anger she'd held so close to her heart since Uncle Patrick's death came tumbling down, as she poured out her heart to God until there was nothing left but questions about what her future would hold.

Since Casey didn't have any tours booked, Amy had given her some time off. Casey would have rather been out on the trail, because, as time passed without contact with Jake, her life felt more and more empty.

It didn't help that Amelia and Gregory were spending almost every waking moment together. Even when he'd drop Amelia off at the end of the evening, the dewy expression on her twin's face dug deep into Casey, exposing her loneliness.

After two days of hiding in her house, Casey was getting ready to go to the school gymnasium to help with the final stretch of decorations for the reunion Saturday night.

Walking into the kitchen, Casey found Amelia sitting at the dining table, with the newspaper laid out in front of her, a mug of coffee in her hands and still sporting her robe.

"We're finishing the decoration in the gymnasium this morning. Do you want to help?" Casey asked.

She glanced up. "I have plans. Gregory and I are taking the train up to Lake Bennett and back."

"Did you give him an answer yet?"

Amelia sipped from her mug.

The coy smile in her eyes made Casey suspicious.

"You're still stringing him along, aren't you?" Casey asked, suddenly very irritated at her sister for prolonging the guy's agony. Didn't Amelia know how blessed she was to have a man like Gregory willing to be so patient?

Amelia laughed as she set her cup on the table. "I haven't given him a definite answer, but I did as you suggested. We're working through some things."

Her irritation eased. "Glad to know I could help."

Too bad she hadn't followed her own advice and opened up to Jake when she'd had the opportunity. He'd handed her the perfect opportunity when he said he thought she was afraid to admit to liking him. He'd had no idea how spot-on he'd been.

She sighed, snagged her backpack and headed for the front door. No use tormenting herself with should-haves. The moment was gone and probably wouldn't come again.

The house phone rang. Amelia jumped up and grabbed the receiver. Some things certainly had changed. Casey reached for the front door handle, but hesitated when Amelia waved her back toward the kitchen.

"This is Amelia. Hold on, she's right here." Amelia held out the phone with a teasing glint in her eyes. "It's Jake."

Casey's heart did a double beat and warmth

flooded her cheeks. She slowly moved toward the phone and lifted the receiver from Amelia's hand. Trying to calm her heart, she put the receiver to her hear. "Hello?"

"Hi, Casey. I hope I didn't catch you at a bad time?"

His voice sounded strained.

"Not at all. It something wrong?"

"Tucker's plane has been found in the middle of Dezadeash Lake."

Fearing the worst, Casey asked, "Tucker?"

"No sign of him. Search-and-rescue is headed out there now. I'm going with."

"I'll be right there," Casey said, as she mentally went over the supplies she'd need. She headed back toward her bedroom.

"Actually, I need a huge favor of you," Jake said.

"Sure, anything." Casey grabbed her hiking boots out of the closet and sat on the bed.

"Mom and Dad are down in Anchorage this week until Saturday. Veronica thought you'd mentioned having some time off this week. I really need a place for her to stay the next few days."

Kicking off her sneakers to put on her boots, Casey said, "Of course she can stay here. I'm sure Amelia wouldn't mind. When can you bring her by?"

A tense pause stilled Casey's hands. "Jake?"

"I'd rather she stayed with *you*."

Straightening, Casey couldn't believe what he'd just said.

On one hand she was deeply flattered, yet everything inside her screamed to help find Tucker.

"Please, Casey. I can't be out there looking for Tucker while worrying about my daughter."

How could she refuse? "Of course I'll stay with her."

"You're a lifesaver. We can be there in about ten minutes, would that work?"

"Yes." She hung up, feeling a little shell-shocked. She rejoined Amelia in the kitchen. "Veronica's going to stay here for a few days."

"Jake's asking you for favors?" Amelia said, her gaze concerned.

"His friend went missing a month ago and

they just found his downed plane. Jake's going to go with search-and-rescue."

"That's terrible. But why's he going? He's not trained, is he?"

"Jake's funding the operation."

"Ah. Pays to have money," Amelia said.

Ignoring the snide remark, Casey thought out loud. "I'll set Veronica up on the couch."

Amelia tsked. "You're falling into your old pattern, Casey. The reason the men in this town think of you as 'one of the guys' is because you're too accommodating and way too nice. If you want Jake to see you as more than just a friend he can dump his daughter off on, you have to be a little more unobtainable."

"My *obtainablity* has nothing to do with this. I happen to feel honored that he'd entrust his daughter with me," Casey snapped. "Don't you have a train to catch?"

Amelia shrugged and disappeared into her room, leaving Casey wondering if her sister's words were true. Was she too accommodating? Too nice? Why was either one bad? This was a crisis situation. She was doing what was right.

\* \* \*

Casey paced for the ten minutes it took for Jake to arrive in his SUV, then met them on the porch. Veronica carried a purple tote bag over her shoulder. In her skinny jeans and long-sleeve shirt, she looked even more willowy.

Jake had a matching tote over his shoulder. He wore his trail clothes, and his haggard expression showed how upset he was by this latest development in Tucker's disappearance. Dezadeash Lake was miles away from where they'd originally thought Tucker had gone down. What had he been doing that far north in the Yukon Territory?

She greeted her guests and directed Jake to put the bags near the hall closet. She'd find somewhere to stash them later. Was the kid planning on moving in? Casey would have been amused at the number of bags she brought, if the situation was so tense.

"Here's a key to my parents' house, in case she forgot anything," Jake said, holding his hand out to Casey.

Compassion swamped her as she covered his shaking hand with her own. "We'll be fine. You find Tucker."

"I know you will," he said, his voice holding a note of confidence that sent a thrill skating over her arms. "I trust you completely, Casey."

His words wrapped around her heart. "Thank you."

Jake gave Veronica a hug before he departed.

"I'll let you know the minute we have news," he said as he opened the front door.

"Please do."

The lingering gaze he sent Casey's way before shutting the door behind him made her wonder what he'd been thinking, wishing she could have read his mind.

"Is Amelia around?" Veronica asked, as soon as they were alone.

A twinge of envy that the first words out of Veronica's mouth were about Amelia hit Casey square in the chest. "She's in her room getting ready. Amelia and her boyfriend are taking an excursion on the same train we took back from Lake Bennett."

Veronica frowned. Casey could see the wheels turning in her brain.

"She doesn't like my dad?" Veronica asked, her voice full of confusion.

Treading carefully, Casey said, "She does. But as a friend."

Veronica's eyebrows pinched together.

Uncomfortable trying to explain the complexities of grown-up relationships, Casey hoped to deflect the girl's thoughts by saying, "So, I've got to head over to the school and help with the final decorations for my class reunion. And then I was thinking, maybe you'd like to visit the Alaska's Treasures stables?"

Veronica's eyes lit up. "I've never ridden a horse."

"Well, today you will."

After saying goodbye to Amelia, Casey drove herself and Veronica to the school building. Once there, she and Veronica helped secure the thousands of rosettes to the backdrop that would hang from the basketball hoop.

The design was of a yellow road leading off into a rainbow. Casey had to admit the whole theme was a bit juvenile, as Amelia had said. The black-and-white theme probably would have been a better choice.

Casey was glad to see that some of the preteen and teenaged children of the other women were also helping. At first, Veronica stood off to the side, but gradually she'd moved closer and joined in the conversation with the other kids.

At one point, Casey found herself cornered by Delilah Carrington, wearing heels, a short skirt and shirt that made Casey think of pirates, and another woman, with teased blond hair and a tight red outfit that showed off every curve and angle she had. Neither of the women had gone to school in Treasure Creek. "This is a surprise," Casey said. "What are you doing here?"

Delilah gestured toward Renee. "We met in town and she invited us to help." Pulling her friend forward, Delilah said. "Casey, this is my friend, Joleen Jones. I told her it was a waste of time talking to you, but she insists."

Annoyance shot through Casey. She had a feeling she knew where this conversation was headed.

"I sure do," Joleen said in a sweet, southern accent. She vaguely reminded Casey of a young version of Dolly Parton. "I came all the way up here to Alaska, hoping to snag a decent fellow, but it seems all the best ones are already taken or uninterested in a girl from the lower forty-eight. But you get along fine with all the men. They all adore you. How do you do it?"

Gratified to hear she was adored, Casey tried to be tactful. "First, I grew up here, and second, I'm not married or engaged or even have a boyfriend, so really, what do I know? Nothing."

Her sister's words came to her about being too accommodating and needing to be more obtainable, but she rejected the advice. Instead, something that Amy had said came to Casey's mind. "Just be yourself, ladies. If a relationship is meant to happen, it'll happen."

The two women glanced at each other, shrugged and teeter-tottered away in their spiky high heels. They stopped to talk with Renee a moment before going back to helping with the flowered centerpieces.

"That was nice of you," Veronica said, as she came up to stand beside Casey.

"What was?"

"What you said to those ladies."

Pleased by her approval, Casey smiled. "Thank you."

"Amelia wouldn't have been so nice."

Casey laughed. "No, you're right about that."

"You two are very different," Veronica said, in a very grown-up tone.

"Yes, we are."

"Why? I thought twins were supposed to be like one person."

Casey sighed. How did she explain, when she really didn't understand herself? "God makes each person unique. Even twins."

Veronica seemed to digest that, then said, "Are we done yet? Can we go see the horses?"

Laughing at her youthful impatience, Casey nodded. "We're done. Let's go teach you how to ride a horse."

Casey drove Veronica to the Alaska's Treasures stable, where they housed the six horses used for mounted scenic tours and for guide support.

As they entered the stable, Casey said, "The first thing any self-respecting horsewoman learns is how to groom her horse."

Veronica wrinkled up her nose. "Does it always smell like this?"

"Yep." Stopping at the stall of a beautiful quarter horse named Beau, Casey said, "Manure, hay and horse sweat. You'll get used to it."

Beau stuck his nose over the edge of the half door and nuzzled Casey's hair. She reached up to pet him. "This young fellow is one of my favorites."

"Can I touch him?"

"Of course. Just keep your fingers away from his lips. He nips."

Veronica tentatively stroked the big brown gelding's head. "Can I ride him?"

"No, I think we'll start with a mellow horse." Casey led the way to a stall at the far end of the paddock. A gray Appaloosa mare whinnied a greeting. "Hi, girl. I have someone I want you to meet."

Taking the halter and lead rope from the peg hung on the outside of the stall, Casey opened the door and stepped inside. "This is Junebug."

Veronica stayed just outside the stall door. "It's awfully small in there."

"That's why I'm bringing her out." Once she had the halter in place, Casey led Junebug out and tied the lead to a railing bolted to the stable wall. "Grooming a horse gives a you time to bond and lets the horse get familiar with your voice and your touch."

Casey gestured with her head for Veronica to follow her to the tack room, where she pulled out a bucket with several soft-bristled brushes with a green stripe painted on the back. "Take one of these."

Veronica did as instructed.

Pulling out a different bucket full of medium-bristled brushes with a red stripe on the back, Casey said, "And one of these."

"Two brushes?"

"The one with the green stripe is for the head and the red is for the body." Walking back to Junebug, Casey instructed Veronica on how to brush the horse. "Use gentle strokes around the eyes and ears. Talk to her as you go so she knows she can trust you."

When Veronica didn't move, Casey held out her hand. "I'll show you." She demonstrated, while cooing softly to the mare. "You're a good girl. So patient."

When she was done with the head, she turned to Veronica and gestured to the brush still in her hand. "Now you can do the body. Start at the neck and brush your way back. Always keep one hand firm placed on the body as you go. This lets her know that you are close."

"Will she step on me?"

"No." Casey watched as Veronica eased toward the horse but kept herself an arm's distance away. "You can move closer. And talk to her."

Taking a half step in, Veronica said, "Nice horsey. You're really big." The brush stroked across the horse's hair. "I like how your feet are brown." Veronica glanced up at Casey, her gaze seeking approval.

Casey smiled and nodded encouragement, happy to see the young girl relaxing as she continued to brush and talk to the mare as she would a friend.

When Veronica finished Junebug's body, Casey showed her how to clean the hooves.

"What is that gunk?" Veronica asked, pointing to the stuff Casey was removing from Junebug's front hoof.

"Mud, manure and mushy feed which probably spilled out of her trough."

"Yuck."

"You want to try?" Casey asked, holding out the hoof pick.

"Another time."

Finishing with the hooves, Casey grabbed a saddle from the tack room and then explained the steps as she went through the process of saddling the mare.

"I know it seems like a lot to remember," she said, as she buckled the cinch. "But over time it becomes second nature."

"Did your parents teach you all of this?"

"No. My parents died when I was six. My uncle taught me how to ride." She recalled those precious lessons with fondness, and amazingly, no grief tainted the memories.

Veronica bit her lip. "Dad told you that my mother died."

Holding the girls gaze, Casey inclined her head. "Yes, he did."

"She wouldn't have liked horses."

"Not everyone does," Casey replied, her stomach sinking at how out of her depth she was with the direction the conversation was heading.

"I have pictures of my mother. I used to want to be like her. Glamorous and special. But she wasn't a very nice person. It was very selfish of her to leave Dad and me."

Casey's eyebrows rose slightly. Had Veronica heard the conversation she and Jake had had in her kitchen?

## Chapter Thirteen

Treading carefully in unchartered water, Casey said, "Sometimes people don't make the best choices."

"She trapped my dad into marrying him," Veronica stated, her eyes big with tears. "I heard Grandma and Grandpa talking. Grandma said Daddy would have done more with his life if my mom hadn't purposely gotten pregnant." A tear slipped down her cheek.

Compassion filled Casey and she pulled her into a hug, even as her mind tried to come to grips with the revelation that Natalie had deliberately gotten pregnant. Why hadn't Jake mentioned that? She thought back to their conversation. Jake was a man who took responsibility for his actions.

"Your daddy loves you very much, and I know he wouldn't change anything if it meant not having you as his daughter."

"You really think so?"

Easing her back to look her in the face, Casey said, with certainty in her voice, "I know so."

Wiping her tears, Veronica said, "Can I ride Junebug now?"

Marveling at the resilience of youth, Casey said, "Of course."

By the next afternoon, Casey was pleased with Veronica's proficiency with the horses. The girl sat astride Junebug and successfully loped around the corral. "That's it. Perfect."

Veronica's wide, beaming smile warmed Casey's heart. The girl was a natural in the saddle. If Casey hadn't known better, she would have thought Veronica had been riding her whole life. The girl hadn't even complained when Casey insisted they muck out Junebug's stall last night before calling it a day.

They'd spent a relaxing evening watching a Disney flick and eating pizza. And this morning, when Casey came out of her room Veronica was dressed and raring to go ride.

As they were leaving the house, Jake called to say they were heading back and would arrive late afternoon. They'd had no luck in finding Tucker. The disappointment and worry in Jake's voice stabbed at Casey's heart.

While Veronica exercised Junebug in the corral, Casey prayed for Tucker. And for Jake's peace of mind.

Veronica brought Junebug to a walk and steered her to the fence railing. "Can we go out?" Veronica asked, with a nod toward the forested mountains and the trails.

"Sorry, your dad will be back soon. We need to get Junebug cooled and groomed, and then I've got to stop by the printers and pick up the name tags for the reunion, and then drop them off before we meet up with your dad at my house," Casey explained, having realized soon into Veronica's stay that the young girl responded well to full explanations.

"Okay. Just one more time around?"

Veronica's coaxing grin made Casey laugh. She was so adorable, with the helmet covering the top of her head, her strawberry-blond hair braided over one shoulder and her cheeks pink from exertion.

Casey couldn't resist. "One more time."

An hour later, after giving Junebug a good grooming, mucking the stall and rewarding the mare with some carrots, Casey hustled Veronica into her Jeep. They stopped by the house to clean up and then ran to the printers. When they arrived at the school, Casey was surprised to see so many cars parked in the lot.

Inside the gymnasium, Renee and several other women were busy putting together corsages. Casey recognized them and nodded a greeting.

Renee smiled when she saw Casey. "Oh, good the name tags. There's a table set up in the foyer where you can lay those out."

"I'll do it," Veronica offered, holding out her hand.

Pleased, Casey relinquished the stack of name tags. "Thank you."

Veronica flashed a smile and hurried away.

"Isn't that Jake Rodgers's daughter?" Renee asked. "She's been with you an awful lot."

"It is. Jake's been out of town, so she's staying with me."

The speculative gleam in Renee's eyes made Casey uncomfortable. "I didn't know we were doing corsages." Casey said, eyeing the pretty yellow carnations. "Did we have money in the budget for those?"

Renee grinned. "Compliments of your sister. She had the flowers flown in, and provided all the ribbon and pins."

Stunned, Casey said, "Wow, that was… thoughtful of her."

"Go figure," Renee stated on a giggle. "I think she was trying to impress the good-looking hunk she was with."

Amelia had been spending a great deal of time with Gregory, and yet, as far as Casey knew, Amelia hadn't accepted or declined his marriage proposal. "You could be right."

"We're all arriving early tomorrow, to greet people as they arrive. You're welcome to join us," Renee said.

Since she really had no intention of attending the reunion, Casey hedged. "Thanks. I'll think about that. I better go see how Veronica's doing."

She found Veronica setting out the preprinted name tags on a linen-cloth-covered table. "You about done?"

"I don't see your name," Veronica said. "I've looked twice, but I can't find a tag with your name, only Amelia's."

"There isn't one."

"Why not?"

Lifting a shoulder, Casey said, "I'm not going."

"What?" Confusion drew Veronica's eyebrows together. "But you've worked so hard to make the decorations and stuff. Why aren't you going?"

Casey wasn't sure how to explain, but she knew she'd have to try or the girl wouldn't relent. "I see everyone I want to see practically every day. This is more for people who've moved away."

"But maybe those people would want to see you?"

A cynical snort nearly escaped. If anyone thought of her at all, it was because of that article. "I'll think about it. We should get going."

The whole way home, Casey endured Veronica's repeated questioning of her decision not to attend the reunion. As she pulled into the driveway of her house, Casey finally said, "Enough. Okay. I said I'd think about going."

Veronica blinked and nodded. "Sorry."

Gentling her tone, Casey said, "No worries. But let's keep this to ourselves, okay?"

Just then, Jake's SUV pulled alongside Casey's Jeep. Without answering Casey, Veronica jumped out the car and ran to her father.

"Daddy, I rode a horse!"

Jake's deep laugh, as he caught Veronica in a tight embrace, tugged at Casey's heart. Pleasure at seeing him flowed over Casey. She hadn't realized how much she'd missed him—or how much she wished she were free to run into his arms, as well.

Forcing herself to turn away, she headed into the house. She didn't want to admit to what she was feeling. The tender and over-whelming emotions filling her made her heart pound and her palms sweat.

She didn't know what to do.

She stood in the middle of her living room, staring at the mess Veronica had made with her clothes and her magazines. Tears sprang to her eyes. She didn't want her to leave. She didn't want either one of them to go.

Behind her, Veronica's happy chatter alerted Casey they were coming into the house, giving her time to compose herself. With a smile in place, she turned just as they walked through the door.

"Gather your stuff, Veronica," Jake said, his gaze steady on Casey. "Thank you. She seems to have had the time of her life."

"We had a good time." She moved to touch his arm. "I'm sorry about Tucker."

Blowing out a breath, he said, "I'm not giving up on him."

"Of course not."

He trapped her hand on his arm, shifted closer, crowding her space. "What's this I hear about you not planning to attend your reunion?"

Shooting Veronica an exasperated glare, Casey said, "Some people talk too much."

Veronica blinked at her innocently. "I never promised not to tell."

With a sigh, Casey acknowledged that fact with a nod. "No, you didn't."

"Why aren't you going?" Jake pressed.

She grimaced. "If you must know, I just

can't stand the thought of having everyone make fun of me."

A thunderous frown marred his handsome face. "Why would anyone make fun of you?"

Surprised to see how upset that made him, she said, "You heard about the magazine article that has brought all the tourists into town, haven't you?"

"Yeah, sure. I didn't read it, though. But that's why there's a glut of females roaming the streets."

"Well, the article also mentioned me, and not in a very flattering way."

Anger darkened his eyes. "What did it say?"

Helpless to halt the flush of embarrassment heating her face, she said, "The article said I was no threat to any of the women in town, since all the men consider me to be one of the guys."

He tucked his chin in. "That's ridiculous."

She blinked. "Why?"

His expression softened. "Casey Donner, you are a desirable and beautiful woman. And if anyone says otherwise, I'll have to beat them to a pulp."

A different sort of heat chased through her. She didn't know how to respond to his flattering words. "I—thank you."

"Daddy, you should take Casey to her reunion," Veronica said, excitement in her tone.

Too startled by Veronica's suggestion, Casey's mind reeled. Shaking her head, she started to object. "Oh, that would be too much to—"

Jake pressed his finger tip to her lips. She blinked at the compelling intensity in his gaze and the slow, playful smile tugging at the corners of his mouth. "I'd be honored to escort you to your reunion."

"Yea!" Veronica clapped.

Casey's gaze shot to the giddy girl and then back to the handsome man whose gaze, and the soft pad of one finger, held her hostage. How could she refuse, when every fiber of her being wanted to jump, leap and soar with joy?

Slowly, she nodded.

"Good." Jake removed his finger. "What time should I be here tomorrow?"

Finding her voice somewhere between her

heart and her lungs, she managed to squeeze out, "Six."

He grinned. "I'll be here."

And then he and Veronica were gone, leaving Casey a quivering mess of nerves. What had she gotten herself into?


"Hey, shouldn't you be getting ready?" Amelia said, as she barged into Casey's bedroom. She wore a tank-style, clinging red dress that flirted with the straps of her matching high-heeled sandals crisscrossing over her slender ankles. She'd twisted her hair back into a jeweled clip. Her pouty red lips turned down into a frown.

"I'm ready," Casey replied, and finished tying the laces on her newest pair of boots.

Amelia's eyes widened, and then a pinched expression took hold of her face as if she'd just eaten a sour lemon. "Uh, no you're not. You are not going like that."

Rising from the edge of the bed, Casey held her hands out. She had on her best and newest microfiber black pants and a soft blue sweater. She'd even left her hair down, but had tucked a band in her pocket in case she got too hot. "This is me."

"But you have a date," Amelia said, in a tone that suggested Casey wasn't aware of the fact, "with a handsome man, who's probably going to show up here in a suit. Because normal people dress up for events like this."

Hating the familiar insecurity tightening her stomach, Casey bit her lip. She didn't have anything else. Certainly nothing like what her sister considered dressed up. "I'm fine."

Rolling her eyes, Amelia grabbed Casey by the arm and dragged her out of her room, down the hall and into Amelia's room. "I have the perfect dress for you."

"Dress?" Casey squeaked.

Amelia sorted through her closet, pushing aside the full hangers until she found what she was looking for. "Here it is." She pulled out a cap-sleeved, royal blue dress with simple, clean lines. "This will look so good on you." She held the dress out toward Casey. "And it's not too frilly."

Casey swallowed back the trepidation that threatened to choke her. "I don't have shoes for something like that."

Amelia arched an eyebrow. "I do." She shoved the dress into Casey's hands.

Holding the garment at arm's length, Casey said, "Right."

Going back to the closet, Amelia came back with a pair of sling-back low heels. "Take them."

With her free hand, Casey accepted the shoes.

"Go ahead, put them on," Amelia said, urging her.

Turning, Casey walked, as if in a trance, to her room. After closing the door, she laid the dress and shoes on the bed and just stared at them. Could she wear a dress? And heels?

She had to admit, the idea of Jake seeing her in something other than hiking pants and thermals appealed to her. He'd said she was desirable and beautiful. She didn't feel either, but maybe she would if she wore this pretty dress.

The sound of the doorbell galvanized her into action.

She made short work of changing out of what she had on and into the dress. The silky fabric glided over her skin, sending an odd sensation cascading down her spine. She felt exposed and uncomfortable with the fabric clinging to her curves.

Slipping her feet into the shoes, she tested walking around her room in the low heels. She was pretty sure she could manage to not fall and break her neck, but the shoes pinched her toes. There was a knock at her bedroom door. She cracked it open to Amelia. "Who's here?"

"Gregory," she answered, with an eager expression. "Let me see."

Casey opened the door wider.

Amelia's pleased smile made Casey stand a bit straighter.

"I knew the blue silk would look good on you." Amelia eyed Casey a for a moment and then grabbed her hand. "You need just a touch of makeup."

"No!" Remembering the last episode with makeup, Casey wasn't interested in having stuff put on her face.

"Trust me," Amelia said, propelling her into the bathroom and forcing her to sit on the edge of the tub. "A dab of lip gloss, a brush of mascara. Nothing heavy or outlandish."

Submitting to her sister's ministrations made Casey antsy. Her foot tapped on the floor.

"Stop that," Amelia groused, as she

approached with the little black mascara wand. "Hold still."

After a moment, Amelia stepped back. She smiled, clearly proud of herself. "Perfect. You're beautiful."

Casey laughed. "Considering we're twins, I'm not sure you should be saying that."

Amelia arched an eyebrow in her classical way. "I have no trouble with the fact that we're beautiful."

The doorbell sounded again.

Casey jumped to her feet. "I don't know if I can do this."

Amelia linked her arm through Casey's. "You can. You're a strong, beautiful woman. And Jake is waiting."

Heart pounding, Casey stared at her reflection. She looked different, yet the same. Not quite like Amelia, whose eyes were smoky with shadow and liner, and whose lips were deeper and filled out with the red lipstick she had reapplied. But close.

Casey just hoped Jake liked the change.

Jake shook hands with the well-dressed man who'd opened the door. Veronica had filled him in on Amelia's boyfriend, which had been good news, as far as Jake was concerned. No more worrying that Amelia would make a play for him again. "Jake Rodgers."

"Gregory Stratton." The tall Englishman stepped aside to allow Jake to enter. "The women are still getting ready."

"Ah."

"Amelia tells me you're in oil?" Gregory said.

"Yes." Jake explained the Rodgers oil history.

"Very interesting. I come from a long line of bankers, myself."

The conversation flowed easily, and Jake found himself really liking Gregory. A flicker of guilt blasted through him for enjoying himself when his friend, Tucker, was still missing out in wilds of the Yukon, alone and possibly injured from his plane crash.

Ten minutes later, the sound of footsteps and a giggle drew his attention to the hallway. The Donner twins entered the room.

Jake blinked in surprise. He had no trouble discerning Casey from her sister—the cautious tilt to the head, the eyes that sought his. But still, the transformation was startling.

He'd considered Casey beautiful before,

with her natural and down-to-earth way. Now she could easily grace the cover of a magazine. Attraction streaked through him, searing him with its intensity.

Gregory's low whistle brought color into Casey's cheeks. "You two will be the most ravishing creatures at this event."

Amelia glided forward and wrapped her arms around Gregory's neck and kissed him on the cheek. "You do say the most wonderful things."

Casey's tentative smile asked a question. Prompted forward by good manners, and not wanting to reveal just how her change affected him, Jake stepped toward her and held out his hand. "You look lovely. But then again, you always do."

She beamed.

And Jake's heart squeezed tight. Natalie dressed to the nines all the time, and not once had she—or any other woman, truth be told—rocked him on his heels like Casey. But he had to keep his wits about him, because now his daughter's heart was involved as well, not just his.

## Chapter Fourteen

Perplexed by Jake's pensive, almost withdrawn mood, Casey tried to draw him out in conversation as he drove toward the high school. But his responses were minimal. Thankfully, Amelia had suggested they ride together, and she and Gregory carried the conversation from their place in the backseat of the SUV.

Casey found her gaze riveted to Jake. He cut a handsome picture in an expensive black suit, stark white dress shirt and thin tie. He'd tamed his hair back. His clean-shaven jaw made Casey sigh, with an urge to run her hand over the smooth skin.

The visceral response pleased and scared her at the same time, and made her glad she'd taken the risk on accepting his invitation to escort her to the reunion.

Finally, when they arrived at the high school, parked and piled out, Casey caught Jake's hand and held him back, allowing her sister and Gregory to enter the reunion ahead of them.

"Is something wrong? You seem upset," Casey asked.

He stared at her for a moment before glancing away toward the snowcapped mountain peaks rising in the distance. "Just hoping Tucker's alive. And safe."

She squeezed his hand, feeling like there was something more, but deciding to accept the explanation. "Why don't we say a prayer for him before going in?"

Jake's startled gaze searched her face. "You'd pray with me? What's changed? Only a few weeks ago, you wanted nothing to do with praying."

"You're right. I blamed God for taking Uncle Patrick from me. All that anger I was holding on to was like a big wall between me and God. Now that it's gone, I feel so much lighter, and open to all God has to offer me. Including the power of prayer."

He captured both of her hands. The look in his eyes, so full of emotions she couldn't decipher, sent her pulse pounding. "I'd love it if you'd pray for Tucker."

Focusing, she bowed her head and closed her eyes. "Lord, we ask for Your protection and covering over Tucker. We ask that he be found soon. In Your son's name, Amen."

When she opened her eyes, she met Jake's amused gaze.

"What?" she asked.

He grinned. "Quick and to the point. I like that about you, Casey."

"I guess I'm a little rusty," she said, feeling a bit flustered, and started walking toward the school.

He entwined their fingers and matched her steps. "The prayer was perfect. You're perfect."

Touched by his words, she tightened her grip. Staring at the wide-open doors of the gymnasium, she said, "I'm not sure about this."

"You'll do fine," he assured her.

Hoping he was right, she took a fortifying breath before entering. She bypassed the name-tag table, because she knew there wouldn't be name tags for her or Jake.

"Oh, wait, Casey," Renee said, catching her before she'd gone too far. She handed her a yellow carnation corsage.

"Hi, Renee. Do you remember Jake Rodgers?"

Renee's eyes widened slightly. "Of course. Hi, Jake. I didn't realize you two were dating."

Jake pulled Casey closer. "It may be a small town, but obviously not that small."

Thrilled by his closeness and his words, Casey stared up into his handsome face. His enigmatic smile left her confused as he led her farther into the gymnasium. Music from her high school days floated on the air as background melody to the conversations taking place among the various groups gathered in the large space.

For a class of fifty graduates, there sure seemed to be a lot of people there. A group of former jocks laughed raucously. Several of the old cheerleaders gathered near the punch bowl. Slowly, with Jake holding firmly on to her arm, they made the rounds, stopping and chatting with former classmates and their spouses. Casey was aware of the curious stares and the whispers trailing behind her and Jake.

"Hey, you two. Picture time," Amelia called, and waved them over to where they waited in line.

A photographer had set up a makeshift photo studio, with backlights and a starry midnight sky backdrop.

Liking the idea of a memento of the evening, Casey turned to Jake, "Would you mind?"

"Of course not," he said leading her over to join her sister and Gregory in line. There were several other couples ahead of them.

"We should do a group shot with all of us," Amelia suggested.

"Sounds good," Jake said.

A couple stepped in line behind Casey and Jake. Happy to be there, Casey glanced back with a smile that died a painful death as she realized who stood there. Seth Davenport. Older looking, and packing some weight around his middle, but she'd have recognized him anywhere. His thick blond hair still curled around the collar of his pale blue button-down shirt. His sharp hazel eyes flickered with surprise.

On his arm was the girl who had been their class's prom queen, Sarah Lender, still pretty in a soft, round way. She'd always been curvaceous. The dress she wore made the most of those curves, and her brown hair was styled in a short bob that emphasized the oval shape of her face.

Casey's heart raced as she whipped her head back around. She hadn't seen his name on the guest roster. He certainly didn't have a name tag. Why had they he decided to show up at the last minute?

"You okay?" Jake asked, his concerned gaze searching her face.

"A little warm."

"Should we step outside?"

"That would be perfect," Casey said, grateful for his consideration.

Amelia grabbed Casey's arm. "No, you can't. What about our picture?"

Leaning close to Amelia's ear, Casey said, "Look behind me."

Amelia's gaze traveled over Casey's shoulder. Her eyes grew wide, then narrowed. Casey's stomach dropped.

"Please, don't say anything," Casey urged.

Arching an eyebrow, Amelia whispered in Casey's ear. "The only power he has over you is the power you give him."

Casey blinked, astounded by the profound words coming out of her sister's mouth.

"Is that Casey Donner?" A female voice asked, rather loudly.

Cringing, Casey shifted closer to Jake. He frowned.

"It couldn't be. She's in a dress."

There was no mistaking the snide male voice of Seth Davenport. Casey wished the floor would open up and swallow her. She didn't want to let Seth have any power over her. Unfortunately, that was easier said than done. Beside her, Jake stiffened. She tugged at his arm. "Let's go outside."

He refused to budge. Then he swiveled to face the man behind him. "You owe the lady an apology."

Seth sneered. "You gonna make me, Rodgers? What are you even doing here, anyway? This isn't your class."

"I'm with Casey." The hard edge of steel in Jake's voice dared Seth to say anything else.

Casey tightened her hold on Jake's arm, even as she threw a glare at Seth.

Amelia stepped around Casey and Jake to confront Seth, Sarah and another couple, who Casey remembered but couldn't put names to.

"Well, well. Look what the cat dragged in," Amelia said, in her best haughty tone. "Sarah. Joyce. I didn't realize the theme was 'Garage Sale' tonight."

Sarah flushed red. "Amelia. Thought for sure we'd never see you again."

Amelia gave an indelicate snort. "Sorry to disappoint."

"Come on, let's come back later," Joyce said and turned on the heels of her pumps.

Casey sagged with relief when Seth and Sarah followed Joyce and her date out of line.

"I'm sorry about that," Casey said to Jake.

He caressed her cheek. "You have nothing to apologize for. That guy was a jerk from day one."

"You have no idea," Casey muttered.

His expression darkened. "Did you two have a thing?"

"Briefly. Ended badly." The admission was weight down her tongue.

Jake's fingers curled into fists. "I should have punched him."

Secretly tickled by his anger on her behalf, she said, "He's not worth it." She met Amelia's approving gaze.

Suddenly, several female screams pebbled the air. Panicked people rushed away from the center of the room, ducking as a small brown bird swooped low and then rose toward the rafters of the gymnasium and back down again, to land on the yellow rosette brick road.

Casey immediately recognized the winged creature by his glossy, furred body and large ears as a little brown bat. Hurrying forward, with Jake keeping pace, Casey shouted, "Everyone stay calm." She needed to keep the animal safe, as well as the people. "Move over to the far side of the gym."

"How do we get rid of it?" Jake asked.

"Find me a container about so big." She used her hands to demonstrate.

Jake peeled away. Casey cautiously moved closer. One of the bat's wings hung at an odd angle. "Oh, you poor baby," she cooed.

The bat lifted its head, its dark eyes on her.

"Will this work?" Jake approached with the box that the name tags from the printer had come in.

"Perfect." She ripped off the lid so that she had a flat piece of cardboard to work with. "Stand back," she advised Jake.

Jake frowned, clearly not liking the situation. "Casey, be careful."

She nodded. Holding the box by the edge with one hand and the flat piece of cardboard with the other, she approached and gently placed the box over the bat, then using the flat cardboard, slipped it between the bat and the paper rosettes. When she was sure the creature was contained, she carried the box outside, away from all the people gathering in the doorway.

She found a low branch of a white spruce tree. Tipping the box on its side, she secured the box against the branch and stepped back and waited.

For a moment, the little animal didn't move, but then the bat used its toes to crawl to the edge of the box, before taking off in flight and disappearing into the night.

Satisfied that the bat was healthy enough, since it flew away, Casey joined Jake on the steps.

"Good job," he said, with warm praise in his tone.

Someone snickered. A female voice rang out, "You can dress her up but she's still just one of the guys."

A hot flush washed through Casey. She halted in her steps. "I can't go back in there."

"Ignore them," Jake said.

She shook her head, feeling like a fraud. She never should have let Amelia talk her into the clothes and makeup. "No, Jake. It's true. This isn't me." She made a gesture to the outfit. "I can't pretend to be someone I'm not. Even for you." She walked away.

"Wait. What?" he called after her.

She didn't stop. Her low heels clicked on the sidewalk as she broke out into a run. All the fears and doubts she'd been trying to ignore stampeded through her like a herd of elk.

When she reached the edge of the school she skidded to a stop. She couldn't run home in these horrible shoes, and she wasn't martyr enough to sacrifice her feet to the gravel roads.

The pounding of male feet behind her drew close.

Steeling herself, she faced Jake as he halted beside her. "Could you give me a ride home, please?" she asked, with as much dignity as she could.

Peering at her closely, he replied, "Sure. After I've had my say."

"There's nothing to say, Jake. This was a mistake. I knew it would be."

He cradled her face in his hands. "Casey, I love you the way you are. Tomboy and all."

She sucked in an amazed breath, staggered by his words and by the love shining in his dark eyes.

His thumb rubbed over her lower lip as he continued. "And you look great in a dress, but you look great in your cargo pants and plaid shirts, too. What you wear doesn't matter. It's who you are here…"

He pressed the pads of his fingers to the exposed skin above the edge of her dress. "The person you are in your heart is the person I'm in love with."

Stunned to hear his words, Casey's mind

scrambled with reasons why a relationship with Jake wouldn't work. All her objections were trite and silly, when faced with the declaration of his love.

An answering love filled her soul and surged through her heart. She wasn't second to her sister. She'd learned she wasn't less of a woman because she wasn't a girly girl. And she certainly wasn't held captive to the anger of the past any longer.

No more isolating herself. She was free. Free to love Jake, regardless of the risk.

"I love you, too," she said, in a voice chock full of love and joy. "I just was too afraid to admit it."

"I know the feeling." He drew her into his arms. "But together, Casey, we'll have a lifetime to chase the fear away."

Rising on tiptoes, she entwined her arms around his neck. "I like the sound of that."

He dipped his head, drawing closer. "Me, too," he murmured, and captured her lips.

She sighed with pleasure as he deepened the kiss. *Finally,* her heart whispered. *A love of my own.*

"Oh, there you two are," Amelia said, as she and Gregory came down the walkway.

Frustrated at her sister's timing, Casey reluctantly pulled away from Jake. "We're a little busy here."

Amelia flashed a grin. "So I see."

"Maybe we should talk with them later," Gregory stated, with an apologetic grimace.

"Talk with us about what?" Jake asked, tucking Casey against his side.

Amelia snuggled close to Gregory and held out her left hand. A large, square-cut diamond twinkled on her ring finger.

Casey clapped her hands. "You said yes!"

Amazingly, Amelia blushed. "I did. We're going to fly to Vegas next month."

Casey tucked in her chin. "You're going to elope?"

"Yes," Gregory answered, his gaze on his fiancée. "That's what Amelia wants."

Amelia held up her hand. "I know you'd want me to get married here, but I've always dreamed of a wedding in Vegas, with all the dazzle and excitement that goes with it."

That was so Amelia. "Then that's great."

"And I want you to be my maid of honor. Will you fly down?"

There was a hint of vulnerability in Amelia's tone.

Casey pulled her out of Gregory's embrace and hugged her. "Of course I will."

Amelia squeezed her tight for a moment, before stepping back. "And of course, you're invited, Jake." She smiled coyly. "In fact, we could make it a double wedding."

Embarrassed by her sister's brashness, Casey squeaked, "Amelia. You're getting way ahead of yourself."

Clearly unashamed, Amelia shrugged. "Just a thought." She took Gregory's hand. "Let's get that picture taken and then blow this pop stand. I could go for one of Lizbet's strawberry milkshakes."

"We'll be right in," Jake said.

Casey stared after her sister, too self-conscious to face Jake. She certainly didn't want him thinking she was rushing him to the altar, though the thought of marrying him sent vibrations of glee sliding over her skin.

Jake's hands gently caressed her shoulders, adding to the sensations coursing through her.

"So, what do you think?" he asked.

Her breath hiccupped. "What?"

He turned her to face him. "What kind of wedding have you always dreamed about?"

Gazing into Jake's handsome face, she said, "*Tomboy,* remember?"

He laughed as he shook his head. "Not in that dress. Besides, even guys think about the day they take themselves off the market." He reached up and tucked a strand of hair behind her ear, his gentle touch electric. "So what kind of wedding do you dream of?"

Without any coyness, she answered honestly. "When the day comes, I want a Treasure Creek wedding, surrounded by the people I love."

"'When the day comes,'" he repeated, softly.

The intensity in his gaze held a secret light that made her pulse pound and hope flare for the promise of a bright future together.

Sliding her arms around his neck again, she said, "Where were we before we were interrupted?"

"Right here," he murmured, and kissed her.

## Epilogue

After church services a week later, Amy enlisted Casey's help to put flyers up around town for the upcoming Christmas pageant. The flyers had information on volunteering, as well as the list of planned activities. Amy believed that getting the word out early would generate more excitement about the event. She really hoped it would be one of Treasure Creek's most memorable pageants. For her sake, Casey prayed so, too.

As they walked through town, posting the informational flyers, the sky seemed bluer and the air fresher. Casey smiled to herself. Everything seemed brighter and more vibrant since the night she and Jake admitted to their feelings. Over the course of the week, Casey was formally introduced to Jake's parents and immediately loved them. The Rodgers were kind and loving and so welcoming that Casey already felt like part of the family.

Casey was getting what she'd wanted most, a love of her own, a family. She slid a glance at Amy as they crossed the street toward Lizbet's Diner. Casey hoped that one day her friend and mentor would find love again. They entered the eatery and weaved their way toward the back of the restaurant, to the community bulletin board mounted on the wall.

Several "hello's" were called out by patrons eating their after-service brunch. Casey waved to Gage Parker, his new girlfriend Karenna, Gage's grandmother and Karenna's cousin. Casey had met her once about a month ago, right after she arrived in town.

As Amy tacked up a flyer on the bulletin board, Dr. Alex Havens walked up with a sheet of paper in his hands.

Casey smiled a greeting. "Hey, Alex."

"Hi, Casey, Amy." Alex smiled, but fatigue darkened circles under his blue eyes.

"Everything okay?" Amy asked, concern lacing her voice.

"Sure. Why?" he countered as he used a

pushpin to tack up a Help Wanted sign. The advertisement claimed the Treasure Creek Clinic was in need of a nurse.

"You looked stressed," Casey said.

He nodded. "I still haven't found my replacement, and without a nurse, I'm pulling double duty."

"You sure you won't reconsider and stay on when your contract is up?" Amy asked.

Regret and something else crossed Alex's features, but before he could give them an answer, Karenna's cousin approached. Tall, pretty, with dark brown hair cut into a pageboy style that framed her oval face. She wore indigo jeans and a pink turtleneck that accentuated the color in her cheeks.

After flashing a smile and quick greeting to Casey and Amy, she turned her attention to Alex. "Hello. Are you Doctor Havens?" she asked.

Casey and Amy exchanged a glance. From the look in Amy's eyes, she was thinking exactly what Casey was: another bachelorette sniffing after Treasure Creek's most eligible bachelor. Many had tried over the past few months, but so far the good doctor had managed to stay single.

Alex drew back, his gaze wary. "I am."

"I'm Maryann Jenner," she said, and stuck out her hand. "I'm Karenna Digby's cousin. I understand you are in need of a nurse."

Casey hadn't seen that coming. She raised an eyebrow at Amy.

Alex blinked. "I—yes, I am. I just put up a Help Wanted sign. How did you know?"

"It's a small town, Doctor." Maryann blew the fringe of bangs from her eyes. "I'm qualified. Really."

From her purse she pulled out a bundle of papers and handed it to him. "My resume, with letters of recommendation from my previous employer."

Alex flipped through the pages. "Highly recommended," he murmured, before carefully refolding them and handing them back. He ran a hand through his chestnut hair, his eyes a bit glazed with surprise. "Everything looks in order. Sure. You're hired. When can you start?"

Relief entered Maryann's pale brown eyes and a smile softened her expression. "Now."

A smile tugged at the corners of Alex's mouth. "Tomorrow is soon enough. The clinic opens at seven."

"I'll be there," Maryann said, with a nod, and walked back to join her cousin and the Parkers.

Watching her walk away, Alex shook his head. "I guess that's that. God does provide in mysterious ways." He nodded a goodbye to Casey and Amy before striding out of the diner.

Casey reached up to unpin the Help Wanted sign. "He doesn't need this anymore."

A speculative gleam shone in Amy's bright blue eyes. "No, he doesn't. I think he found everything he's looking for."

With a laugh of agreement, Casey crumpled the flyer in her hands. She had a feeling Doctor Alex Havens had just met his match. Too bad he wasn't planning on sticking around long enough to figure it out.

\* \* \* \* \*

*Want more Treasure Creek? Look for Alex and Maryann's story,* DOCTOR RIGHT, *by Janet Tronstad, available in September from Love Inspired.*

Dear Reader,

I hope you enjoyed this latest installment of the ALASKAN BRIDE RUSH. Though Casey longed for love and a family of her own, she was too afraid to jeopardize her heart, because of the hurts of the past. But in Jake she found a man worth risking it all to love. Jake certainly never expected to find a bride, especially a local tour guide, but how could he resist down-to-earth Casey? Especially when his daughter fell for her, too?

Though Treasure Creek, Alaska, is a fictional town, the Chilkoot Trail is a very real part of American and Canadian history. In researching the backpacking trip that Casey leads Jake and his daughter on, I discovered a world I knew nothing about, and sparked a desire to one day travel to Alaska to hike in the footsteps of the Klondike miners.

Coming next in the ALASKAN BRIDE RUSH series is Dr. Alex Haven's story. Stop by and see what mischief the residents of Treasure Creek are into now.

Blessings,

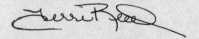

# QUESTIONS FOR DISCUSSION

1.  What made you pick up this book to read? Did it live up to your expectations?

2.  Did you think Casey and Jake were realistic characters? Did their romance build believably?

3.  Talk about the secondary characters. What did you like or dislike about the people in the story?

4.  Was the setting clear and appealing? Could you "see" where the story took place?

5.  What type of vacationer are you? Do you prefer to be active? Would a hike in the Yukon appeal or do you prefer sitting on the beach with a book?

6.  Casey was angry at God because of her Uncle's death. Have you ever felt this way? How did you come to terms with the feeling?

7. In her first romantic relationship Casey felt pressure to compromise her faith. Can you tell of a time when you have been faced with a situation where you felt pressured to bend to the world's ways rather than God's? How did you resolve it?

8. When Jake thought Veronica was lost, he realized he really communed with God only in a crisis and vowed to talk to God every day. Do you talk to God every day?

9. Casey and Amelia had a strained relationship. Do you have a sibling? Can you talk about your relationship?

10. As a single parent, Jake second-guessed his decisions on his parenting. Can you tell of a time when you've second-guessed your parenting?

11. Did the mystery of the Treasure Creek treasure pique your interest? Any guesses as to who might be after it?

12. Notice the scripture in the beginning of

the book. What application does it have to your life?

13. How did the author's use of language/ writing style make this an enjoyable read? Would you read more from this author? If so, why? Or why not?

14. What will be your most vivid memories of this book?

15. What lessons about life, love and faith did you learn from this story?